D1086493

Zhang Tianyi (1906-1985) was a Chinese left-wing writer and children's author, whose novels and short stories achieved acclaim in the 1930s for his satiric wit.

David Hull has translated numerous short stories from Chinese. His translation of Mao Dun's novel *Waverings* received a PEN/Heim Translation Award. He is an assistant professor of Chinese Language, Literature and Culture at Washington College.

Zhang Tianyi

The Pidgin Warrior

A Novel

Translated from the Chinese by

David Hull

Balestier Press
London · Singapore

Balestier Press
71-75 Shelton Street, London WC2H 9JQ
www.balestier.com

The Pidgin Warrior
Original title: 洋泾浜奇侠
Copyright © Zhang Tianyi, 1936
English translation copyright © David Hull, 2017

First published in English by Balestier Press in 2017

ISBN 978 1 911221 09 8

The Pidgin Warrior

Contents

Preface

BIG BOYS, THE STORY in this little book is told for you.

If I said, "Long ago there was a king..." or, "Long ago there was a monster..." you would shake your head and wouldn't listen: Ah, others are so much older and still listen to those stories!

It's true, you are already so much bigger. Hearing about some Aladdin's Lamp or old Soldier's Tinderbox does nothing for you. What you like to hear are adventure stories and swordsman stories. Ha! especially the swordsman ones. "Adventure" is actually an import: foreigners want to find a place where they can make money, that's why they get into that line. As for swordsmen—foreigners have them too of course. But they can only cross swords using force against force: At best, a man like d'Artagnan might hold off ten or so and be considered top-rate. But they can't fly over the roofs and climb walls. They can't they leap to the top of a ten-thousand foot mountain in one bound either. And as for spitting secret blades out of the mouth, "in a glimmer of light, a head hits the ground," well, that's not even worth asking!

The abilities of the Chinese swordsmen are truly remarkable. You know this of course: You've read so many illustrated storybooks about swordsmen: *The Seven Heroes and Five Gallants, Little Five Gallants, Seven Swordsmen and Thirteen Gallants, Seven Swordsmen and Eight Gallants,*

Jiangnan Gallants, and all the rest…

And so you read yourselves into a rapture. In the past few years a couple of little children even snuck out of their houses and tried to go Mount Emei to seek the Dao.

There are adults who have read themselves into a rapture over novels about swordsmen too. But they don't abandon their wives and children to go off somewhere seeking the Dao, because adults are somewhat more mature than children. They just daydream about it in their minds or talk about it emptily with their mouths, but that's it. This business of swordsmanship is too murky, no one knows where to go to learn it.

No one even knows where to go to see it, much less to learn it. Among all of our friends and people we know, there isn't one who is a swordsman. No one has seen a swordsman. Or if they have, they've only seen them in those characters in the illustrated storybooks—each and every one dressed up like a stock military *wusheng* on the stage, although they are a lot of fun to watch flying back and forth from the roofs of the Wing-On or Sincere Department Store.

Everyone has heard there are immortal swordsmen at the top of Mount Emei, but the people who live at Mount Emei believe the immortal swordsmen have always hidden away at Mount Zijin or Mount Tang or Mount Kun.

But there are some people on the side who are laughing to themselves. And they are truly much more important than the immortal swordsmen. We've been talking for all this time—completely forgot to mention them. They are the mothers of the swordsmen. The swordsmen were born out of their bellies. They close their eyes and think for a while (Perhaps they might not even need to think at all), and with a giggle they give birth to an outstanding swordsman. With clasped hands, they go to the boss at the bookseller and collect their draft fee. That's nowadays of course. As for those of earlier generations, those trailblazing ancestors who told swordsman tales, they didn't have any draft fees to collect. They just wrote them out and gave them to friends for amusement and nothing more.

The people they wrote them for—they are a group of people who are called "unofficial agents" in the novels, or they come out of the "unofficial agents." They always end up running into difficulties in life: Sometimes they just aren't allowed to live a peaceful life, and sometimes they get tricked—someone gets over on them somehow. Even though the law of the land exists, there are places where the emperor can't reach. So they make up a person with great skill to come and help them. What humans can't do, these fantastic people can. They have the morality of the agents, they understand ritual propriety and they understand the position of the agents. They assist those in the service of the emperor, like the Judge Bao and Judge Peng types bringing peace and stability to the land, eradicating bad guys and allowing the agents to live a comfortable life.

And even more than that, these people of great ability are incredibly generous. As soon as there is a problem, they fly right over—help out for you, go to great effort for you, without you spending a fraction of a penny. If you offer to give them a real send-off, they won't let you. It's so much better than even those officials Zhang Long and Zhao Hu from *The Water Margin*.

The more these stories are told, the more they progress. If it was only a swordsman laying waste and slaughtering bad guys, without running into any tougher opponents his entire life, that might seem to be a bit monotonous. So, from among the pack of bad guys will emerge an "Evil" swordsman to do battle with "Good." They start with eave-jumping and wall-climbing and progress to spitting out secret blades from their mouths. The result—of course, you could figure it out on the first guess—the "Good" of the agent is victorious. If they aren't victorious, then they can go and seek instruction form those immortals of the "True Doctrine." Because the immortals will help the true Son of Heaven and their agents. On telling the story or hearing the story told, people who think like the agents, or those who have been educated by the agents, will all glow with happy smiles: Everyone is utterly happy, it's true!

Among them there are also some—a little more earnest, who actually come to blows and want to struggle against this group on their own. He wants to become a swordsman himself. And so he…

This little book of mine will tell of just such a man. Here—I want to explain why our hero wanted to go study such a peculiar profession, how he came to study, and after completing his study, what things he wanted to do.

(For anyone who might want to become a swordsman—please do not neglect this: This little book might be said to provide a "How-to guide to becoming a swordsman." Reading this is just as good as what someone studying how to write a novel would get from reading those *How to Write Fiction* books.)

But my story here doesn't mention everything: and it might lead you not to understand several points. Otherwise, what would I be doing nattering on bothering you with this revelation?

This will serve as a preface.

—The author, April 1936

1

Arrival in Shanghai

A sleeping city. A peaceful night.

Suddenly...Boom!

Whoosh!

The artillery shell swept through the black sky with a whistle, and then—Bah-boom!

The XX munitions factory was blown into a crater. It was a Sun Brand shell.

The second barrage followed. Rifle reports. The third barrage. The fourth. The fifth.

The sleepers jumped out of bed.

"What!..."

"It's some kind of live-fire exercise again, right?"

"It doesn't sound like it."

"They're always having those live-fire exercises!"

"Listen!"

Someone screamed out. The massacre had already begun.

"XX devils!"*

"What are our soldiers doing?"

But they had decamped to XX!

That information quickly spread. Every corner of the city shook as if in paroxysm. Every wall was covered in

---

* Here and elsewhere, Zhang Tianyi follows the convention of the time to refer to potentially sensitive place names as "XX." This is particularly common when referring to Japan or Japanese people.

announcements. On the streets the cry shouted out, "Extra! Extra!" The air was awash in nervous talk.

"They're going to be in Tianjin soon!"

"Beiping is in a difficult spot too."

"Kill every last devil!"

"Chaos is here now!"

"What'd they have the soldier retreat for?"

It was like the entire world was a rubber band pulled taught. With just a slight bump, it snapped with a pop.

"It had to happen sooner or later."

"Our kind of people have to find a way out for ourselves!"

Students became active too: grabbing flags and heading out to the Dongdan Archway, shouting. People on the streets felt this time the students were a bit different than before: This time the events would impact even them.

"Good kids!"

"Everyone go!"

Some people ran all over the place trading information:

"Are things really dire here in Beiping?"

"Who can say?"

"I'm thinking of moving back south. Are the banks still allowing withdrawals?"

They all spoke softly, as if a raised voice would be heard by the devil soldiers. Their breathing was strangely labored: the atmosphere had congealed thicker than paste long ago.

"Elder Shi Bo, what's the news you've heard like?"

"Untenable. The stratagem is: "Against Overwhelming Odds: retreat.""

"Exactly so, exactly so. I'm still going to go over toward the bank to see if I can hear some news."

The bank was busy handling withdrawals for its clients. The auction house had a couple dozen people coming by every day to have cumbersome furniture they couldn't take with them appraised. At the station, telephone calls were coming in, flustered faces were coming in, all wanting to reserve places in first and second class sleeping cars.

"Alright. It's all settled."

And so cars swarmed out of Qianmen, stopping at the entrances of the East Station and the West Station to disgorge their contents: Wives, concubines, bedding, jujube boxes, elder masters, ladies, leather luggage, young masters, chausie cats, biscuit tins, male servants, rattan baskets.

On sitting down in the sleeping car that felt like a bathhouse, a sigh.

"Relax."

"But Tianjin? Who can say if Tianjin might be all in chaos. That would be a disaster."

The sitting person smoked, calmly watching the others squeeze onto the car. A porter, his head jammed awkwardly to the side by some leather cases or something was struggling and calling out:

"Pardon! Pardon!"

Behind the porter the owner of the leather case squeezed in, anxiously looking around. His two legs only briefly stopped moving and the bedding that was coming up behind him pressed into his neck.

"Pardon! Pardon!"

"Quickly, quickly, the train is getting ready to leave!"

Everyone had found their berths and quietly awaited the train's departure. Everyone had their legs splayed out, strolling out of the little compartment door walking through the hall. Everyone would certainly run into a couple of friends in the car.

"Elder Shi Bo!"

"Ah! Mister Liu Liu!"

"Please, come in and have a seat."

That one called Elder Shi Bo who had a few wisps of a beard strode through the little compartment door.

"Going to Shanghai?" Mister Liu Liu pulled a cigarette from a green foreign metal case to give to that Elder Shi Bo.

Elder Shi Bo nodded his head, popping the cigarette into his mouth and moving to take advantage of the light in Mister Liu Liu's hand.

"And Bao Juan?" Mister Liu Liu asked.

He rapidly took in a few mouthfuls of smoke and blew the smoke out which freed his mouth to say, "We all came together."

In the compartment, aside from Mister Liu Liu, there was a forty-ish fat man who had been smiling and staring at Elder Shi Bo the whole time. Mister Liu Liu glanced at the fat man, and felt he had to do something about it.

"Have the two of you met? This is Elder Shi Bo, ah, Mister Shi Boxiang. And this is…"

"I've very much looked forward to meeting you," the fat man dashed out. "You have lived in Beijing for quite some time, Elder Shi Bo?"

"Jiachen… Yisi *…Oh… nearly thirty years."

Everyone was given a sudden jolt as the train began to move.

The Elder Mister Shi Boxiang took a drag on his cigarette, but it had gone out.

"Has Brother Dashi come along with you?" Mister Liu Liu

---

* Jiachen is 1904, Yisi is 1905. These dates are based on the "stem and branch" calendar system.

asked the Elder Mister Shi Boxiang as he glanced around, as if looking for that Brother Dashi. He looked under the seat and then the ground, then put his hand in his pocket and dug around.

"Oh, he also came with us."

Mister Liu Liu found his matchbox and gave the Elder Mister Shi Boxiang a light. And, looking at the fat man, "Elder Shi Bo's son Dashi's martial arts are quite good. He's... He's... What was the name of the school? It had a name. Was is the Shaolin School?"

Elder Shi Bo smiled. "I can never keep those names straight either. He was... It was called some kind of internal gongfu, right?"

"Does he still practice every day?"

"He loves to play around with that, and I don't bother him much about it. He was concentrating some kind of qi. Horseplay, that's all it is!"

The fat man stuck out his belly and told Elder Shi Bo in a loud voice that the skill concentrating *qi* was an extraordinarily powerful skill in the martial arts.

Gan Fengchi was one who could concentrate his *qi*, Gan Fengchi! His voice raised even louder — he worried that the sound of the train would drown his voice out.

"As long as you are willing to work hard, there's nothing that can't be learned well. Has your honorable son been formally accepted by a master?"

The Elder Mister Shi Boxiang opened his mouth and was about to reply, but the fat man kept up his questioning rapid-fire.

"What is your esteemed son's courtesy name?"

"Zhaochang. The first character Zhao is "omen" as in 'a bad omen,' and the Chang? Chang... Chang is... It's "prostitute" but without the female part. *"

"Will you allow us to meet?"

It seemed like the fat man was an expert in these things. The Elder Mister Shi Boxiang looked at that fat swollen face, and then strode out of the compartment into his own to call his eldest son Shi Zhaochang over.

Shi Zhaochang was a half-head taller than his dad, and maybe twenty-five or -six years old. The corner of his eyes pointed up, which made him look like an actor in an opera. His face was red and he was bit pudgy. His chest was quite developed, but he did all he could to suck in his belly, which gave him a bit of a hunched back.

The youth greeted Mister Liu Liu and the fat man with clasped hands. He sat down on the seat and hunched his back even more.

The fat man stared at Shi Zhaochang. "What type of gongfu has Brother Shi been practicing of late?"

"Form-Intention Boxing"

"You must have practiced a long time."

"Half a year," Shi Zhaochang took the cigarette offered by Mister Liu Liu. "It's actually not that difficult. My teacher says that practicing gongfu relies entirely on whether or not you have a natural-born foundation. If you don't, no matter how hard you work, you'll never get it right. That makes a lot of sense."

The fat man nodded. He wanted to ask more about how his gongfu exercises were going, but he couldn't make out if Form-

---

*   The name is 兆昌. The first character means "omen." Elder Shi Bo has trouble explaining the second character, finally explaining that it is like the character 娼, but without the part on the left that represents female. With the female radical, the character means "prostitute." 昌 by itself means "prosperous" or "flourishing."

Intention Boxing would be categorized as external gongfu or internal. He looked out the window: the countryside flew behind them.

Half to himself, he said, "Internal gongfu is very important."

Shi Zhaochang was startled. Oh, this fat man might know a couple of things.

He felt him out: "I also practice the skill of concentrating my *qi*."

The fat man turned his head back, puffing out his belly, and started talking in a loud voice about Gan Fengchi again: "You should train qigong like Gan Fengchi's. Gan Fengchi was truly outstanding. For example… For example…"

He looked around to see if everyone was paying attention to him, and then went on to talk about Gan Fengchi.

"Gen Fengchi showed his ability in the presence of Emperor Yongzheng: He pulled a thread… a hair… a… a thread… Ah… it was a thread…"

That's right, it was a thread. He said the thread was fifteen *zhang* long. He said Gan Fengchi took that thread, and concentrated his *qi*. Puffing out his belly again, he said thread stood up, like a perfectly straight bamboo pole — fifteen *zhang* tall.

"And that's not all." The fat man stood up and started gesticulating. "At the very tip of the thread, that's fifteen *zhang* high, on the top of the thread, he had a golden ingot weighing five thousand *jin* placed up there. Ah! Now that's gongfu!"

Shi Zhaochang tapped the ash off of his cigarette and asked, "A five thousand *jin* gold ingot?"

"Yes. It was Emperor Yongzheng's. However…" At this, the fat man's voice become calm and even, and he sat himself down. "However, that that's nothing either. Afterward, Gan Fengchi told Emperor Yongzheng to have all of his warriors come and pull on the thread. So five hundred warriors came to pull…"

Of course they couldn't move it. And the fat man smiled in victory.

Shi Zhaochang breathed out a long breath. A lungful of smoke floated over toward the fat man. He had exhaled with a bit of force, and he looked at the fat face opposite him—to see if the face showed any discomfort from his smoke.

But the fat man didn't mind at all. He just puffed out his belly again started telling a story about concentrating the *qi*…

Elder Mister Shi Boxiang and Mister Liu Liu were discussing the current events.

"I wonder if there is trouble in Shanghai."

"There shouldn't be any." Mister Liu Liu said calmly.

Elder Mister Shi Boxiang threw away his cigarette butt, and pulled another from the green foreign metal case. He crossed his legs, his back leaning against the wall. After making himself comfortable like this, he took a long sigh. "The Chinese people really have no fighting spirit! Look, since… since, since… since that…"

Mister Liu Liu seemed to not have been able imagine someone might suddenly express such emotion. He stared emptily for a while before understanding the topic that he was raising.

"Yes." Mister Liu Liu glanced at the Elder Mister Shi Boxiang, before shifting his gaze to a rattan basket. "This time those befuddled people truly seem set on destroying the nation. Those so-called…so-called…and yet… but it seems… Everyone feels that this nation isn't their own."

He smiled knowingly. "You and I haven't the strength to truss a hen. We could struggle with all our might to no effect. We would be better off… in any case…Ah… A man of wisdom must protect himself first. And yet… And yet…"

Suddenly his son burst out enthusiastically, "Not so! Not so!"

The Elder Mister Shi Boxiang was startled, and with another "And yet…" he stopped.

But the fat man said peaceably, "Of course, I know better than you."

Ah, what were the two of them arguing about?

Shi Zhaochang continued, his face reddening.

"The warriors who have skill with swords are much more powerful than ordinary ones. Of course, Lü Siniang was a swordswoman, an immortal of the blade, she was… If she were an ordinary warrior, she never could have assassinated Yongzheng. She killed Yongzheng with a spitted blade."

"You misremember," the fat man spoke each word slowly. "Lü Siniang's skill was in wall-climbing and flying over roofs, not in blade-spitting. She was a warrior, not a swordswoman."

"Impossible! I've read the books…"

"Of course, I understand these things better than you, ah." He made a gesture to quiet others down. "Of course, I understand these things more clearly than you. No one knows Lü Siniang better than I do. There is also a familial relationship between Lü Siniang and I."

Shi Zhaochong was startled, his eyes staring widely at the fat man.

The fat man slapped his knee, and spoke in quite proper manner about that familial relationship: "Her elder brother's son's sister's son's great-grand daughter's husband is one of my cousin's mother's brother's brother's son's sister's husband's aunt's son. So I understand Lü Siniang's situation better than anyone. She was certainly no immortal of the blade."

"If she were an immortal of the blade, then she would have

been more..."

"Of course immortals of the blade are more powerful," the fat man worked his hands together.

"In any case I should get to this point in my studies, otherwise I would have wasted my whole life." Shi Zhaochang looked out the window, "one must study the Daoist Arts to be an immortal of the blade."

The Elder Mister Shi Boxiang broke in, "For that one must have native ability. How do you match up?"

The youth looked askance at his dad and swallowed.

Mister Liu Liu placed his hand on the youth's shoulder. "You see those..."

Shi Zhaochang flushed throughout his entire body. His heart beat loudly, shaking nearly to shatter his chest.

"Without martial arts, China cannot be saved," he said, panting, short of breath. "We only need one! ... would we fear the devils then? ... must learn swordsmanship!"

The Elder Mister Shi Boxiang recalled the words Lü Dongbin said when he spoke through spirit possession at the altar: China cannot be destroyed because a great hero of national salvation reached maturity and must soon appear to undertake great things.

Was that hero his own elder son Shi Zhaochang?

He didn't think so. If that great hero did come out of his family, he hoped that it would be his second son, Shi Zhaowu—Now that child had native ability. He didn't care much for his elder son.

Shi Zhaochang looked at his dad and threw the cigarette at that green foreign metal case with all his might. He knew the old man didn't believe in his elder son. Ever since his stepmother gave birth to Zhaowu, the elder son immediately became a something that could be taken or left. The old man felt that the elder son didn't have anything great in terms of prospects. But of course, Shi Zhaochang himself knew so much more about his future than that muddleheaded old man.

"Humph. You just watch!"

He looked again at his dad. His dad pulled out a handkerchief folded into a rectangle and used it to dispassionately wipe his three or four wisps of beard. Ever since he had married his stepmother, his dad's face had become a loathsome visage: Hmm, look at those malicious, demonic eyes!

This entered into dark magic, it did! Actually the old man was quite good. But as the two of them made it back to their own compartment the old man chided Shi Zhaochang: One should not boast about oneself.

"Boasting will never get you anywhere."

"What was I boasting about?" Shi Zhaochang didn't look at his dad.

"For example right then when you were next to Mister Liu Liu…"

"A man will always have his ambition," the son said loudly. "To talk about one's own ambition isn't boasting."

The Elder Mister Shi Boxiang stared for a while.

"Ambition…" the old man muttered, rubbing his hands.

"Dad, don't be difficult with me all the time. I know you are… Ah, never mind."

"What?" His tone became oddly friendly.

"Younger brother is utterly lost in the dark and yet you never chide him."

"Your younger brother is going through a muddled phase. What can I do?"

"Ah, a muddled phase," the son smiled.

The old man simply believed in the younger brother.

The fortune-teller said that he would become a division commander by the age of sixteen. The old man took his younger son as a *Taisui*. *

"Hm, division commander by sixteen!"

To be fated to become a division commander by sixteen wasn't actually that strange, it was just that Shi Zhaochang didn't believe that he could do it: his younger brother just didn't have it in him.

He couldn't sleep that night. The train rumbled along. It wasn't easy to practice gongfu on the train. He hadn't done his evening exercises.

Why run off to Shanghai? Frightened?

Could he find a master in Shanghai? But those immortal swordsmen and men of the Dao wouldn't stay in Shanghai. Those people were always up in the Kunlun Mountains, hiding away in dark obscure huts, refining their inner alchemy, concentrating their *qi*. If not there, at Mount Emei…

Shi Zhaochang sighed and rose, lighting a cigarette.

"I've got to think of a way to get to Mount Emei to seek the Dao."

He had heard that if he wanted to go to Mount Emei, Shanghai was at least a bit closer than Beiping. After learning the Dao, it would take one day of work to clear out the bandits, and then he could go and take back the three northeast provinces and force the capitulation of the XX nation. A little rest, and then he could go on to conquer other nations: Russia, England, and some of those Javanese nations.

"The United States?"

He thought for a long while: The United States was quite friendly to us Chinese. …Eh, he could wait until the time

---

* Demigod.

came to decide.

Then, everyone would know there was a Shi Zhaochang. Every family in China would erect memorial tablets for his longevity, kowtowing and burning incense. He would need a lover, a woman like Thirteenth Sister. He would do good deeds together with his lover.

Shi Zhaochang puffed on his cigarette with determination.

Perhaps he would be able to find a woman like Thirteenth Sister in Shanghai. There was a book called… called…

"Called what?"

Called, yes, called *Something Something Predestined*. Exactly, he went looking for her over in Tianqiao. He went to Tianqiao, but couldn't find her: those performing martial arts were nothing but some male heroes. There was only one area with a woman, and that was a sixty or seventy year old woman. Damnit, there was only one woman like Thirteenth Sister in Tianqiao: the one in that book!

In the few days and nights he was planning these things, he didn't speak to anyone. The old man didn't understand him. His mother-in-law simply didn't get along with him from the beginning. Zhaowu was muddleheaded. He was just by himself, smoking, lying back, and planning what to do first when he got to Shanghai.

"I'm not at all familiar with Shanghai."

He'd never been to Shanghai. The person who had been taking them to Shanghai had left. He had to get to know some new people.

Even though he had been in the train several days, he wasn't tired. Others were red-eyed, stepping off the train as if in a daze. He just mumbled a few words, grabbed his leather case and jumped down to the platform, landing right in front of someone's face.

The platform was crawling with people like ants.

Were there enough people here for him to find a friend?

Ah, Shanghai!

That night, Shi Zhaochang strode out of the hotel onto the sidewalk of Avenue Edward VII.

His hands were fists and his jaw was set tight. He strode out repeatedly on the cement in a splayfoot stance, eyes peeled with attention at every face.

"Aya," an angular face called out to him suddenly, "My Savior! The Great Warrior! How did such a man as you come to Pidgintown? When did you arrive, good sir?"

But Shi Zhaochang had forgotten who the angular face was.

"Don't recognize me?" he said, bending at the waist in something like a bow. "I am Hu Genbao... Where's the good sir's hotel at?"

"Ah, perfect!" Shi Zhaochang's eye lit up. "I'm staying at a hotel run by a Hunanese man. We're moving tomorrow or the next day. How have you been? Weren't you..."

2

The Child of a Splayfoot Culture

IN THIS WORLD, there are many fortunate things that come about by chance. Dear reader, you must know that I speak of Shi Zhaochang. Shi Zhaochang was just thinking of getting to know a few people in Shanghai. And then? Hu Genbao.

Last year Shi Zhaochang—no, it was the year before last—the year before last, he met Hu Genbao in Hankou. He was walking over near Jianghanfu where a few guys wearing short blue coats surrounded someone in a lined gown and were attacking him. The man was trying to appease them, bowing and begging, but he was still taking it on the chin. Shi Zhaochang walked up and pushed through the blue coats:

"Get out of here! I'll flay the next man who lays another hand on him!"

"What's it to you!" the blue coats said. "This man Hu sold us, he..."

"I dare you to make another move!" He immediately dropped into a horse stance, looking solid.

It goes without saying that among those lower class guys there wasn't one worth anything.

I don't recall if there actually was a fight, or if a police patrol came by, but to make a long story short, those surrounding the man in the lined gown were broken up.

"Truly you are my benefactor," the gowned man bowed. "If it weren't for your arrival, my life would have been in danger. What is your honorable surname?"

"It was nothing. I am Shi." He saluted with cupped hands.

"Please come to my home to clean up. Your honor has…"

"Think nothing of it. Fighting injustice is my duty."

"You are truly a great warrior. This world today…"

With this he had made friends with the gowned man, and that was Hu Genbao. But their friendship hadn't lasted long: not long after that, his father had sent for him to be brought back to Beiping.

"Ah, I never thought I would run into you here!"

On the sidewalk, men and women walking hurriedly brushed by them. A few people selling late editions and children selling tabloids yelled out wildly.

And yet Shi Zhaochang stood there the entire time, telling Hu Genbao what he had planned.

"Are you familiar with Shanghai?"

"I'm an old Shanghailander," Hu Genbao smiled so that his entire face was wrinkled.

"In Shanghai, I would like to find a…"

"A little place to eat. Your honor probably hasn't eaten. Allow me to serve as host."

"Ah, no," Shi Zhaochang made a firm gesture with his hands. He felt that he should put out some capital at this time. "I'll treat."

Hu Genbao's back gradually straightened as he blew out a breath.

"Yes, yes. What kind of restaurant does your honor prefer? There is a Zhejiang place here."

"That will do fine."

"Over wine, Hu Genbao told Shi Zhaochang that he knew a lot of people.

"And there are some that are quite impressive."

"You mean good at martial arts, do you?"

"Martial arts? Humph, good enough that you could go to heaven and still not find one to best him."

Maybe it was an immortal swordsman. Maybe it was one of the Dao. But Shi Zhaochang feared getting his hopes up only to be disappointed, so he said calmly, "Most likely is someone with internal gongfu."

But Hu Genbao shook his head. With a strange politeness, he stopped sipping his wine, the flesh on his sharp face shaking.

Shi Zhaochang's eyes fixed on Hu Genbao's eyes. Damn him for keeping him in suspense.

Hu Genbao picked at his teeth, cleaning his mouth before finally saying that this wasn't an ordinary man.

Then he jumped up, nearly overturning the table.

"Ah!?"

A tea server stood respectfully at their door.

"What," Shi Zhaochang said. "Could it be? Could it be?... Ah!"

"Yes. But it must be steamed first," the tea server said.

"What. We're speaking of our affairs, what is it to you!" Then, "Old Hu, who is it?"

Shi Zhaochang's body began to float. What kind of man would Hu Genbao said it was? Who was it?

"If the Supreme Ultimate Master were to come to Shanghai..."

"Of course I would introduce your honor. He said that within a month a man was going to come and ask to be taken in as his student. This person would have native ability. He also said he would be from the north."

"He... He... He..." Shi Zhaochang was so excited that he nearly fainted. His butt hit the chair and his face flushed. "How did you come to be able know the Supreme Ultimate

Master?"

He wiped grease from his mouth with the back of his hand. "I bowed to him at the sacred altar and took him as my master."

"You…You…You… What? You are his disciple too?"

"It was early this year that he become my master. He teaches me the Daoist Arts. Would you like a little pepper? The Supreme Ultimate Master is… If you don't eat the duck it will go cold."

Shi Zhaochang stared at Hu Genbao's mouth. He had started speaking before he had finished swallowing the duck soup and the liquid, with something that looked like foam, had trickled down his chin. This Hu Genbao was studying the Dao. But the Supreme Ultimate Master said that someone was coming to bow to him and take him as master. Who was that? Who was that?

"I want to study the Daoist Arts. All swordsmen must understand the Daoist Arts."

"The Supreme Ultimate Master does."

"And Passing Through Earth…?"

"He knows it all, he knows it all."

Suddenly, Shi Zhaochang stood up and took one long stride to Hu Genbao and made a formal bow with clasped hands.

"If you… If you… do you respect me?"

"What? I…" At this surprise, he stood and retreated a step.

"If you respect me, I… I… Let us be sworn brothers!"

The tea servant brought in hot towels, so the oaths to swear brotherhood had to be delayed for a moment.

As the two walked out of the main door to the restaurant, Hu Genbao burped as he caught up to Shi Zhaochang, calling him Second Brother.

"Second Brother, how about we go to The Great World?

Second Brother, I'm so full, oh! Second Brother, tomorrow we should…oh… tomorrow we should go to the Commercial Press Bookstore to buy the *Directory of the Golden Lotus* to formalize our oath. When you move out, I'll help you move. I'm… oh! Second Brother, Master will be here soon. You just have to wait, Second Brother. The Master is…"

"Ah!"

Shi Zhaochang waited anxiously for a week.

"Elder Brother, will the Supreme Ultimate Master truly come?"

"Don't be impatient. The Master said he will come. He will come."

"Elder Brother, Do you think the Supreme Ultimate Master will take me?"

"Second Brother, relax. Just leave it to me," he said patting him on the chest.

"Elder Brother, what kinds of gongfu have you studied? Can you tell me a little bit?"

"Eh? Eh… Eh! I just started," This elder brother reached out to the cigarette tin, but it was empty.

"Liu Fu! Go buy a tin of cigarettes. Liu Fu!"

Hu Genbao looked at a lithograph printing of a set of couplets in Qing Daoren's calligraphy that hung on the wall. Each and every character seemed to bend like rattan. Between the couplets hung a rubbing of an engraved image taken from somewhere: "In Memoriam, Yue Fei, Prince E of the Song." Hu Genbao raised that angular face to stare at the rafters.

"Second Brother, how much is this house per month?"

"I think it's seven hundred fifty *liang*. I really have no idea."

"The house isn't bad at all," Hu Genbao looked out the window. "And it's big enough for your whole family?"

Shi Zhaochang wanted to talk more about studying the

Daoist Arts, but his Elder Brother was hung up on asking if the house had a bathroom, did it have a flushing toilet, as if he was going to be practicing Daoist alchemy in the bathroom.

What was he always asking those things for? In brief, they lived in a house—three floors, seven hundred fifty *liang* per month. They moved in five days ago.

"Who all lives in the two garrets?"

From the kitchen downstairs, there was a sudden noise: crack!

Shi Zhaochang curved the edges of his mouth downward. "Humph. Playing mahjong again. If all the Chinese people were all like those, we'd really be done for."

"I should go pay my respects to your father." He rose in a stretch.

"No need. You don't have to be so polite. You're my Elder Brother. I won't hide anything from my Elder Brother. My family is…"

He told his Elder Brother: Having his family was like not having a family. His birth mother died when he was three. When he was eight, his father married a woman and they had Zhaowu. He was utterly alone. His mother was very sharp, and saw this coming. Before she died, she had her husband set aside some money to save for their son. Of course, the family had money besides, but there were bandits out there and there was no relying that he could get it in his hands.

"Now, the only relationship I have with my family is that money. The rest of it has nothing to do with me."

"How much money is it?" His Elder Brother asked offhandedly. "Is it all for you to spend on your own?"

"Eh. I'm an adult. I can use the account however I like. It's really not that much, only three thousand and some change. I haven't touched it. I'm preparing for a great undertaking."

"Your father and you…"

"Eh, don't bring that up." Shi Zhaochang exhaled. "He's a good man really, but he's entered into the dark path.

To be honest, his father seemed to have a grudge against him. His father and step-mother stood to one side and teased him, made fun of him. He knew that second wife of his father's harbored nothing good toward his father: she was looking forward to his death so that her own son would be the sole recipient of all his assets.

Look! Even the people in his own family harbored such suspicious minds!

"Eh, there aren't many good people nowadays!"

Isn't that the truth—everything you see and hear is all evil people hurting good people. All the big shots just do all they can to squeeze out rent and grain. And don't those damn foreigners just casually murder a few ordinary Chinese folks just for fun? The rich trade in foreign rice to the point that you can't get any price for Chinese rice. The tenant farmers are getting more and more rebellious, and it will end up on the heads of their landlords. Dammit, can this be tolerated? And the past few years there have been bandits riling things up in the countryside, and the fucking XX devils, too?

As for Shi Zhaochang, he had to be a hero: What he had suffered, what others had suffered, he had turned it into outrage. He had suffered, but he also thought of what others had suffered.

"Yeah, I've got to be a hero."

What his father had said long ago was so true: "You were born with the horoscope of a general. You must study hard, understand? You must study hard. Do not be an ordinary person."

Everyone said that his horoscope fated him to be a man of

astonishing accomplishments.

"Come." His father had often dragged him in from of him. "Tell me. What kind of person are you going to be?"

"I will be Guan Yu. I'll be Yue Fei."

"Good boy!" He would clap. "Then your father will be proud."

He read *The Loyalty of Yue Fei*. Then he read *The Seven Heroes and Five Gallants* and *Seven Swordsmen and Thirteen Gallants*. He started to study martial arts. This was all when he was young. But he never changed: he still thought of his future, still bowing to a master and studying martial arts.

But now his father had transferred his hopes to Zhaowu and didn't have faith in his eldest anymore.

"Hmph. I must be stalwart… I must… It is mandated by fate. It's my native ability.

To be a hero, one must believe in oneself. One must train tirelessly. One must establish great ambitions.

Last year, on passing his twenty-fourth birthday, he found a run-down temple to Guan Yu and he made a vow. He knelt before the red-faced god with wrinkled brow.

"I will practice the Dao until I am transformed into an immortal of the blade. I will scour the world clean of evil men and fight all injustice. I will subdue the entire world. I will annihilate all Evil—Those who don't believe in gods, those who don't respect the Dao of the sages, anti-Confucians, those who don't maintain the separation of superiors and subordinates, those who promote communal wives, those evildoers. I will kill every last bandit, I will capture every last thief in the world…"

Now he thought about it to see if he had left anything out. As so he added another: "I will make our land peaceful in life and happy in work, grain will be affordable, the lower classes will enter into the Way of Good and will know the difference between superior and inferior, they will know their own place and will have faith in the heavenly decrees of fate. I want to bring peace to the world. I, Shi Zhaochang make these vows and I am resolute in my ambition: Please, Duke Guan…Please Lord Guan… Please Elder Guan… Guan Guan Guan…"

He suddenly didn't know how to address him.

What, forgotten? Didn't Elder Guan become an emperor after he died?

"Please Emperor Guan!" He said quickly. "I, Shi Zhaochang plead to Emperor Guan for your blessing on my success… I, Shi Zhaochang pledge my life to become such a swordsman."

He had actually made these vows long before, but up until that day he had never formally made the pledges before the face of the god. And so he had to do all he could to find a man of the Dao to take as his master, find a master of martial arts who could teach him Form-Intention Boxing.

"That type is only a foundation gongfu," Shi Zhaochang said as he opened up the newly-bought tin of cigarettes. "I've studied several forms."

As if reciting a memorized resume, in one go, he told his Elder Brother the other forms he had studied, and then put a cigarette in his mouth. *Thus Endeth the Curriculum Vitae.*

Hu Genbao kept staring at the rafters.

Silence. From downstairs came the sound of mahjong tiles and laughter.

Shi Zhaochang paced up and down the room: He used the splayfoot stride of the masculine characters from the opera. His eyes were always fixed on the big mirror on the wardrobe: watching to see if his bearing was correct or not.

His father taught him this splayfoot stance when he was small.

"People who are Correct walk in a Correct way. Don't be all higgledy piggledy."

His father walked around with a splayfoot stride to show him.

"Walking must be done like this with regular precision. In ancient times, the sages, the emperors, the ministers, the generals, they all walked like this. Monks and Daoists use this stance when they do their rituals. All you have to do is go find someone who has studied the Way, even today, they walk with this regular precision. Even though walking is a small thing, you must pay close attention. In our China, this nation of propriety, this stands as a... a kind of... a kind of... Well, anyway this type of bearing represents our cultural legacy."

Correct people absolutely walk with this type of stride. Even though he had never himself seen those ancient heroes or great warriors, from watching operas and from what he had studied carefully in paintings, he saw: Guan Gong, Yue Fei, Hua Mulan, Wu Song, Jiang Ziya, Thirteenth Sister, Dust Mote, Zhuge Liang, Gan Fengchi, Laozi, they all had this same splayfoot stance, and many, many more people too.

Who knows if Supreme Ultimate Master had legs like that too...

Shi Zhaochang's eyes slid down from the big mirror, settling on the two legs of that disciple of the Supreme Ultimate Master.

His legs were folded, nothing to be seen there.

"Brother, how does the Supreme Ultimate Master walk?"

"What?" He puzzled.

"Ah, nothing. I was just..."

Suddenly a girl cried out from downstairs, "Mom! Mom! Second brother pulled my hair! Mom!"

Shi Zhaochang immediately rushed out the door.

He was going to right an injustice, right?

No. That little girl was the fourth sister of his stepmother. She was always at odds with Zhaowu and had just come to lodge her complaint with her mother. This wasn't uncommon.

But downstairs in the guest room the wet nurse was making accusations against the second master too:

"You see Mistress, Second Master stole one of my pairs of trousers and threw them in the trashcan. Second Master beat me too, look. Look Mistress."

The Mistress' voice: "What? Your trousers?"

The men and women who were playing mahjong roared in laughter.

Dear Readers, you have not seen that Mistress, so you will allow me to introduce you. Come downstairs and take a look at the commotion.

Ah, now that one with the purple scar on her temple is the wife of the Elder Mr. Shi Boxiang, Shi Zhaochang's stepmother. In age, she doesn't look more than forty. Her eyes are reddened. Sitting behind her the Elder Mr. Shi Boxiang is looking at her tiles.

The wet nurse is standing in front of them, with the not quite one-year-old fifth sister in her left arm, her right arm stretched out to show her the black-green bruising on her wrist.

"How could he have run off with your trousers?" Mistress kept her laughter-induced tear-filled eyes locked on her tiles.

"The dresser in my room is broken. Second Master just went in, snatched them, and ran. He threw my trousers in the trashcan. I came to tell you Mistress, Second Master just beat me."

Mistress wrinkled her brow slightly.

"What a muddle of a wet nurse you are: you can't even

babysit your own trousers! You are all aware of Second Master's temperament. You should be more careful. What a person, you!"

Then Mistress sighed. "That boy Zhaowu is certainly naughty. Even if someone can't babysit their own trousers, you shouldn't throw them in the trashcan, trashcan...Pong! Seven wan pong! Three bamboo. You'll eat that one I bet. Three bamboo is a good one, and I've just broke up a pair to give it to you. You don't want it? Such a good tile and you don't want it? Truly naughty. It infuriates me. Trousers in the trashcan... How did Mrs. Liu make a set? Ai, Boxiong, light a cigarette for me. I'll have to punish Zhaowu. Zhaowu! Zhaowu! Where has Second Master gone to? Call him out here...Zhaowu!"

"Spank Second Master! Spank Second Master!" Cried Forth Sister, but her voice was drowned out by the shuffling of the mahjong tiles.

Seven or eight minutes later, Mistress sighed again. "That boy Zhaowu is certainly naughty. Fifteen years old. Aiya, thanks to you for that red dragon! What a good gunner to set off my cannon! Ha Ha ha! Even though they say we should encourage a martial spirit, you shouldn't beat the wet nurse—if you injure her, how would we have milk? And after stealing the trousers, was there any need to throw them in the trashcan? That boy infuriates me!"

The Elder Shi Boxiong cautiously lit Mistress's cigarette and tried to comfort her: "That boy Zhaowu is truly naughty. But don't come down too harshly: When he becomes a division commander at sixteen, won't you enjoy your son's good fortune?"

"Even so, these times always make you a little grumpy, don't they? Now, I'm always...Self-drawn all chow! I've been waiting on a four or seven bamboo for so long. Are you waiting for one? I was waiting on that four seven bamboo forever! I couldn't wait any longer. Right, wait until I'm enjoying his good fortune, but for now he is too naughty. A mother's heart is never at ease…"

Mistress put her cigarette on the ashtray so she could shuffle the tiles, but her mouth kept on. She told everyone about the fortune that was told to Zhaowu about becoming a division commander at age sixteen.

"To be a division commander at sixteen would be a hardship. There would be not time to play around as a division commander. So I'm a little more forgiving toward him now. Of course sixteen is a little too young to become a division commander, but what can one do? But in ancient times, there was an outstanding prime minister who was only twelve. Zhaowu is fifteen this year, so there aren't many days left for him to play around, so let him play. By the end of the year, he will be done with his silliness and in the new year he will begin his proper work. If he wants to play, let him play, he'll never again…again with the…his ambition is in the military realm. But… but… I've always thought to become a division commander at sixteen, will be a hardship. Others are still children at sixteen, ah, isn't that so, Mrs. Liu?"

Shi Zhaochang walked his elder brother downstairs and stood outside the door to listen for a while. He spit heavily on the ground. "Hmph, a sixteen year-old division commander! Like he could!"

3

The Flying Mud-Pellets of the Woman Warrior

THE WEATHER HAD GRADUALLY become colder, but the news was still tense. There was a citizen's meeting at the public sports field. Students flooded the North Station, taking trains to Nanjing to make petitions. Solicitors of donations to the Aid the Northwest Volunteer Corps carried their bamboo tubes around, asking for money. Every national salvation group had mobilized all at once.

Many guests had just arrived at the Elder Mister Shi Boxiang's home. They were waiting for food to be served while they listened to a committee member from the National Salvation Group give a talk.

"I hope that each of you will join our Group, because everyone here is of the elite families."

The committee member looked out the window, speaking as if from a script. The listeners could only see the flat back of his head.

Shi Zhaochang stood and as he went to the table to get the committee member a cigarette, he said, "But I feel that your position is useless."

On this the committee member turned his head back. Dear readers, take a look at his face: ah, it is someone we are already familiar with, Mister Liu Liu.

Mister Liu Liu seemed not to have heard Shi Zhaochang. A cigarette hung from his lips as he took a small volume from his black leather bag.

"This is the charter of our Group."

The Elder Mister Shi Boxiang pulled out his eyeglasses and put them on. First he commented on the cover of the volume:

"These characters are written very well indeed."

Several heads gathered around.

"These are Zhao Style."

"The strokes are a bit similar to Zhao Style, but whoever wrote this certainly studied Zheng Xiaozu's characters."

"Not so. I have a friend, Mr. Le Lezhai, and his characters look a bit like Kang Nanhai's. He studied Wei Dynasty stele writing - the Shimen Stone Carvings by Wang Yuan. Kang Nanhai studied the Shimen Carvings too."

"I don't think so," The Elder Mister Shi Boxiang said with a lingering voice.

"In that case, what do you think the writer studied?"

Boxiang only stared distractedly for a while. "It does have a flavor of Yan in it. I think... I think it... I think it...Perhaps he studied Qian Nanyuan's."

"Qian Nanyuan's—I'm not so sure."

Mister Liu Liu smiled in triumph, without saying a word. He wanted to wait until someone asked him, but he couldn't resist.

The cover of the volume was:

Hunger Strike of the Elite National Salvation Group Charter
        —The Imprint of Le Lezhai, Doctor of Literature

One friend in western attire had seen the characters on the cover clearly and left the gathering of heads and with an older gentleman returned to the sofa talking about Le Lezhai's characters.

"I saw him copying inscriptions with my own eyes. He was copying... Mi... Mi something, Mi Shee... Shi Te, Mi Shite!"
*

"Mi Shite?" The older gentleman didn't understand.

"Hm. With my own eyes, I saw it, with my own eyes! He was copying out Mi Shite's rhapsody on the Great Peng Rhapsody."

Mister Liu Liu rubbed his hands together courteously, and with a loud voice, encouraged everyone to sign and join the Group. "Please, why don't all of you become members?"

He looked at everyone's face, then stood and continued in oratorical style: "The national crisis has come to a head. The elite cannot but come to the salvation of the country... We go on a hunger strike to urge brethren of the entire nation to resist Japan and save the nation. There is power in a hunger strike. In India, didn't that renowned great man, Mr. Tai... Tagore, go on a hunger strike for the salvation of his country? Even the English were afraid of him. As for us... we..."

The orator licked his lips and paused...

"What do you all think? Each of you is one of the elite families in China. If we go on a hunger strike then the brethren of the entire nation will surely be strengthened: It would be no laughing matter for the entire country's great names to starve to death. If all the elite families starved to death, what kind of nation would it be? We would naturally strengthen the resistance to XX and national salvation. Please join, all of you, everyone please stop eating to save the nation."

Shi Boxiang scratched his head and probed, "Does one

---

* Mi Shitte: There is a famous calligrapher of the Northern Song named Mi Nangong (米南宫). If you misread his name, pronouncing it "Mi Tian Gong (米田共)," you have wordplay for the three parts of the character for 'shit (粪).'

have any energy when one is starving? Are you...?"

"I don't eat a single grain." * Mr. Liu Liu answered quickly. "This morning I only had five poached eggs and drank a little tea with chocolate milk. At twelve, I had two bowls of noodle dumpling soup and dough noodle soup. At seven this evening, I did the same. Each day, if I get hungry, I just eat one or two Guangdong mooncakes, and that's enough. Right before bed, I have a little fish porridge with a couple of eggs in it. That's it and nothing more. I don't eat a single grain."

Everyone looked at each other. That friend in the western suit stood and raised both hands high in the air. "The elite cannot but come to the salvation of the country. I plan on joining the Hunger Strike of the Elite National Salvation Group, but this luncheon today... this... this luncheon... We can't snub Old Shi Bo's generosity—this luncheon must be eaten. Everyone can sign up after we eat. But the characters on this book, I saw that Le Lezhai was writing Mi Shite's characters with my own eyes... We'll join after the luncheon."

"The entrance fee is five *yuan*. One year's membership dues are seven *yuan*. VIP membership is thirty *yuan*."

Liu Fu came in to report the meal was ready.

"Liu Fu," the Elder Mister Shi Boxiang recalled, "Liu Fu, tell the kitchen to make two bowls of dough noodle soup for Mr. Liu Liu. Mr. Liu Liu will not eat a single grain... Zhaochang, go upstairs and have the women come down to eat."

Mr. Liu Liu was talking about the Hunger Strike of the Elite National Salvation Group, but Shi Zhaochang kept his lip curled: Other people are of the elite, they look down on him and he looks down on them. Farces like this were damned

---

* I don't eat a single grain: "To eat" in Chinese is literally "to eat rice," So Mr. Liu Liu is able to say that he doesn't eat a single grain, which is identical to how you would say I don't eat: "I don't eat rice."

useless. If...

"Move!" the Elder Mister Shi Boxiang yelled at Zhaowu: The boy had taken the place of honor at the table and wouldn't budge.

The guests stood aside at looked at the table, no one took a seat.

The Mistress ever-so-carefully twisted her hair over her temple to cover her purple scar. With the other hand she tugged at Zhaowu.

"Good boy, you're so obedient. Let the guests sit down."

"No way." Zhaowu said with a cracking voice.

The guests urged the host to let the young master have the seat. But there weren't enough seats. With him there one of the guests wouldn't have a place.

"I don't need to sit," Mr. Liu Liu said. "I'm on a hunger strike. I can eat the dough noodle soup next to the tea table."

Zhaochang wanted to make a cutting remark about his brother, but they fixed the situation by bringing in another chair.

Talk moved from national salvation through hunger strikes to the Volunteer Corps.

"Supposing the elite of the entire nation were willing to go on a hunger strike, the Volunteer Corps would certainly take part too, and the government would immediately dispatch troops."

"But the Volunteer Corps is useless." Shi Zhaochang interjected.

"Those XX weapons are just too powerful. The Volunteer Corps can't do anything against them. We..."

Zhaowu interrupted with a shrill shout, "When I'm a division commander, I'll slaughter all of the XX devils!"

"That younger son sure has spirit!"

"When I'm division commander, I'll lead soldiers to XX and beat them there!

The Mistress began laughing, "It'll be good enough if when next year comes along, you don't forget this spirit."

"If next year when I'm a division commander I do forget, then I'll be dog-fucked!"

"Pei!" The Elder Mister Shi Boxiang spat out.

The Mistress cooed, "A division commander at sixteen might be a little early after all, isn't it? You have to be a little older to go fight the XX. Too young and it would be a little dangerous."

"I'm not worried," Zhaowu chewed his food. "Dad's a disciple of Lu Chunyang.* He can call on him to help me. I'll take the soldiers to fight the XX—Blam! Blam! Blam!"

He mimicked firing a rifle, but as the bullets came out of his mouth with a "blam" something he was chewing fell out into Mrs. Liu's wineglass. Mrs. Liu had been holding her chopsticks, eyeing a chicken dish, but the Mistress raised her glass in toast, so she rushed to put down her chopsticks, raise her glass and drank it down.

The Elder Mister Shi Boxiang sucked at some soup that was in his three or four strands of beard and smacked his lips. Then he told everyone about the events at the temple to Ancestor Lu in Beiping. **

Zhaowu opened his red eyes wide. Hearing his dad's descriptions had him entranced. His eyes popped out like a goldfish's, with little black dots. His face was as sallow as an over-steamed Buddha's hand fruit. His mouth was big, but it couldn't compete with his gums: as soon as his mouth

---

*   Lu Chunyang – Lu Dongbin, a Tang dynasty Daoist mystic.

**   The Temple served as the headquarters of the Boxers.

opened, his huge gums would come poking out.

"Ancestor Lu must help me kill the XX," he shouted. "I want dough noodle soup!"

"Don't make such a racket!"

But Zhaowu had already snatched away the dough noodle soup that Mr. Liu Liu was in the middle of eating. Mr. Liu Liu was startled, and stared at the Elder Mister Shi Boxiang as if asking for help—but the others were talking calmly about how Ancestor Lu had taken him in and even given him a Daoist name, and even written calligraphy for him through a séance.

"That," the Elder Mister Shi Boxiang pointed at a gilded piece of calligraphy on the wall, "that was written by Ancestor Lu."

Mr. Liu Liu thought, "It doesn't matter if I have one bowl less, I'll just eat some fish porridge when I go back."

At this he felt relieved and followed everyone else in looking at Ancestor Lu's calligraphy.

Mistress was afraid everyone might not be able to read the characters near the top, so in a ringing voice she intoned, "...Where the mystery is the deepest is the gate of all that is sautéed and wonderful..." *

"'Subtle,' not 'sautéed.'"

"Oh, 'subtle.' But the grass script 'sautéed' is written just like that. Grass script calligraphy is truly difficult to read, isn't it, Mrs. Liu? I stared at the words at the top for an hour before I figured out what they were. When you get used to it you can read it. When I was at school I learned so many grass script characters. Nowadays at school they don't pay any attention to that sort of thing anymore. The schools are just no good

---

* Following Legge's translation of the Dao De Jing.

now. The people running the schools just have no sense of reason. Zhaowu went to that school in Beiping, Mrs. Liu you understand, I just had no way to deal with them. I said… I say, everyone please don't be polite, please eat a little more. There's not much left. Really, I had no way to deal with them. The school wanted to have Zhaowu held back a year. They said his work wasn't good enough. It's simply interference. I thought, how can they blame our children? He's just going through a confused phase. This is no way to go about things. I told them, "You just handle it. Let him go up a grade, and next year when he comes out of his confused phase, his work will naturally catch up." Hmph! But they didn't understand the sense of it. They won't even talk sense with you! Zhaowu, he'll be a division commander at sixteen, leading soldiers, his fate says as much, that's why I wanted him to graduate from school. If he got left behind a year they he wouldn't be able to graduate before sixteen, and wouldn't that interfere with his future? I said, "Fine. You're running a school and you can't see sense. If there's any interference in our child's future, then it will all be on you teachers' heads!" Hmph, I really gave them a bit of a harsh tongue-lashing… it infuriated me. People don't see sense…Mr. Wang, you know… Ah, Mrs Liu, right? Schools nowadays, ah, really! Like that school we were in: Script, Grass Script, English Letters, even English cursive, Literature, Gymnastics, have to study all of those things! Grass script is terribly important. Zhaowu though, his father had him learn a few grass script characters. Zhaowu, you can read these characters, recite them for us…"

Zhaowu had a mouthful of dough noodle soup and no interest in recitation. He just shook his head.

"That child!" Mistress laughed reproachfully. "All good intentions, I ask you to recite and you won't recite. He also taught his little sister to read grass script characters. When you're an officer you'll have to write grass script too. You'll see. People who deal with official paperwork all write grass script. Before, when Shi Boxiang handled the official paperwork in the yamen he had to write grass script. He had to go through one hundred papers in a day, worked so hard he even forgot to eat. Eat, please eat as you like, there's no need to be polite. Mr. Liu Liu, aren't you a great drinker? Cheers! Finish off that bottle and then keep eating. Once you're done eating, Ah… handling that official paperwork, there's so much paperwork. And in the military there's got to be even more. You won't be able to play like this next year, Zhaowu. And in fighting the XX, there will be more and more paperwork. After you fight the XX, you'll get promoted to brigade commander…"

"A corps commander."

"Ah, corps commander. But a brigade commander and a corps commander are just about the same, aren't they. Fighting the XX, as long as Ancestor Lu is willing…willing to help him…to protect him… so Ancestor Lu said there will be someone to come and save the nation and fight the XX and then go…"

Liu Fu brought in a calling card and showed it to Mrs. Liu: There was a Miss He who wanted to see Mrs. Liu.

The male guests looked to the door. The frosted glass made it so they couldn't see anything.

Mrs. Liu didn't recognize the name on the calling card. She didn't even have time to reply to Liu Fu before the door opened and in walked a woman. She looked somewhere between eighteen and thirty-eight—It's so difficult to figure out the age of a person like this.

Everyone stared at this woman. Shi Zhaochang even shuddered: was this a human or a demon?

"Ya guys don't recognize me?" The woman spoke through a thick Shanghainese accent. "I'm Mi-su* He! He Manli—Mary Ho! *The Southeast Daily* has my pics in it like all the time la! *Illustrated Beauties* does to! Now who is Mi-suh-se Liu la?"

"Mrs. Liu? Here."

"Do you recognize me, Mi-suh-se Liu? You have met Mi-suh-se Wang on Myburgh Road la. Mrs. Wang knows Mi-se-tuo Tao, and I'm friends with him, so I'm your friend too la! I want you to do somethin' for me: introduce me to everyone here la!"

Mrs. Liu's face flushed. She didn't know how to handle this, but that friend in the western suit broke through the difficultly:

"Allow me to make the introductions..."

This Miss He looked everyone over with a smile as she placed her hand on the back of Mrs. Liu's chair so that she could twist her body. Then she looked down at her legs to see if the pose worked or not. She giggled, "Everyone's so... Everyone here is a big wheel patriot la! I came ta ask for your patriotism la! Now, I'm the playwright, manager and public relations manager for the Modern Patriotic Song and Dance Troupe, and I've got one thing to say at ya..."

Shi Zhaochang tugged at Mr. Liu Liu's sleeve. "Why is she saying 'la' all the time? Is that Shanghainese?"

"I don't know."

Miss He's speech flowed out like a waterfall. Now that the XX were fighting the Chinese, the Chinese people must use patriotic song and dance to save the nation, so everyone here

---

* In addition to Chinese titles, He Manli often uses transliterated English: Mi-su for Miss; Mi-suh-se for Mrs.; Mi-se-tuo for Mister.

should buy tickets to see her troupe.

"Now in these times of national crisis, we've cut the price of our admission tickets twenty-five percent! The shows're all fuckin'... They are very good patriotic operas, there's *The Improved Moonlight Evening*. Li Jinhui wrote *Moonlight Evening*, but now I, ya know... improved it. Now Chang'e leads the women's corps to beat the XX bloody! And there's *China I Love You*, that one's just savage good. It's the tune of *Sister, I Love You!* Then there's the *Woman Warrior of National Salvation...*"

"*Woman Warrior of National Salvation!*" Shi Zhaochang was stunned.

"Sure. That show is wicked good la!"

"Woman Warrior!" The young man's face flushed. "Is she skilled?"

"Oh, she's the darb!"

"What?"

"She is very skilled! That's it." Miss He walked over to him. "I would like..."

Miss He moved in closer to him and pulled out an admission ticket to give him. There was an artificial scent about her, so thick he nearly fainted.

Zhaowu suddenly broke out in cackling laugher. "Elder brother's flirting with that girl! Elder brother's flirting with that girl!"

"Little kid's a wicked beast la!" The woman said.

But Shi Zhaochang's face had gone even redder, and he glanced around at the other faces.

"Elder brother's..." Zhaowu was using his hands to imply something.

"Bullshit!" Shi Zhaochang roared.

"Elder brother's flirting... Hahaha!"

Shi Zhaochang stood up abruptly and Zhaowu dove under the table to hide.

"Elder brother is so shameless! Flirting with that…"

The table suddenly jumped up with a bang—dishes spilled all over and wine glasses all tipped over.

"Get out from under there Zhaowu!" The Elder Mister Shi Boxiang called out.

"That boy is so naughty," Mistress smiled slightly. "Hiding under the table was fine, but to give it a bang like that. Look, the table is filthy."

All of a sudden Miss He cried out and jumped back because a hand had poked out from under the table and grabbed her pant leg. From under the table a great cackling laugher rose up.

"Ahahahaha, hahaha… Elder brother flirting… Elder brother flirting… hahaha!"

Everyone broke out in laughter. Shi Zhaochang felt like uncountable millions of ants were crawling all over his body.

"I was… I was…" he stuttered out. "She has the Woman Warrior of National Salvation… without the Woman Warrior, we can't save China… China… so I…"

Miss He, as if forgetting what just happened, said that now the Woman Warrior of National Salvation must absolutely be supported.

"Women're patriotic too, ain't they? So of course we need women warriors, la!"

Shi Zhaochang left the table and saluted Miss He with cupped hands. He was delighted to make friends with her. There was no one in the room that he could speak to. Only this out-of-nowhere warrior was his equal. China could only be saved by relying on warriors. Anything else was fucking useless! Ah. The Woman Warrior of National Salvation! He must pay her a formal visit. He couldn't find anyone like Thirteenth Sister in Tianqiao, but in Shanghai?

He then went on to tell Miss He of his grand designs: What he had studied and what he planned to do.

"I simply must find a girl like Thirteenth Sister and go to fight the XX with her. To fight back against injustice... Tell me is there a way to meet with this Woman Warrior of National Salvation?"

"Well, it's me, ain't it!"

"What?!" Shi Zhaochang put his hand against the wall for fear of falling over.

"I'm the Woman Warrior of National Salvation."

Shi Zhaochang looked her over carefully. How? A person like this is...

Her hair looked permed. There was thick rouge smeared on her lime-white face. Freckles could very faintly be made out. Big red lips. Her collar rose above the bottom of her ears. Her breasts pushed out. Legs like matchsticks.

So thin? But people with internal gongfu could be thin or fat.

"You practice internal gongfu, I assume?"

"Sure!"

"What school?"

"What school?" The Woman Warrior didn't understand.

"There are all sorts of schools, like Kunlun School, like Shaolin School..."

"Oh, I'm in the Romantic School!"

He heard but didn't hear. He quickly made a respectful obeisance to her, and they became friends.

"You can come by and see me anytime!" Miss He smiled charmingly. "Our song and dance troupe would also like to have your donation!"

"Of course, of course."

Shi Zhaochang walked her to the door. She wrote down her address and gave it to him.

"You can call a rickshaw and come visit."

"Dicksaw?"

"Rick Shaw!" She shook his hand suddenly, turned and left.

He stood dumbly at the door for a while. His body felt like it was soaking in boiling water. He watched her back as she left. Then she turned quickly and blew him a kiss.

How, what? Some kind of dart?

But there was no flying blade.

Suddenly something fell upon his head: a little mud-pellet, still damp.

He was stunned. He blew out a long breath and returned to his own room.

"Truly it was excellent gongfu—The mud-pellet was so accurate!"

Hanging out of the third floor window was Shi Zhaowu: After seeing his brother leave, he laughed loudly, then picked up the second mud-pellet and hurled it at a coachman by the street.

4

The Subjugation of the Cook

IF MUD-PELLETS HAD the minds of scholars, there would certainly be some fatalists among them. Just as with mud-pellets, fates are different. For example, the second mud-pellet that Shi Zhaowu's threw fell next to a coach. When the coach departed, it was crushed underneath. Early the next morning, the street-sweeper swept up its corpse and buried it in the garbage can. But the one that fell on Shi Zhaochang was so much more fortunate: it was ever-so-respectfully picked up by Shi Zhaochang and then carried upstairs into his room.

Shi Zhaochang stared at it for five or six minutes.

It was a very ordinary mud-pellet: Yellow, a little damp, soft to the touch. Ah, luckily it wasn't hard. Otherwise it might have raised a huge lump, or even taken his life. But of course it couldn't. The woman warrior had just displayed a little skill for him to see. Someone cared for him a great deal.

He pulled a brocaded box from a case, took out a piece of jade that was inside, and placed the mud-pellet in it. He looked around then, clasping the box, he walked to his bed with the stride of a Daoist presenting a treasure before hiding it under his pillow.

Outside, the wind blew. The window shutters were blown open and closed, the room suddenly dark and then suddenly light. The memorial portrait of Yue Fei that hung on the wall jumped, and then a long wind blew in, bending the portrait out like the arch of a bridge. This made Yue Fei's stomach stick out so high it looked like he was pregnant.

Shi Zhaochang's brows furrowed as he glanced at Yue Fei and went to close the window. But the latch was broken, it wouldn't close.

On the balcony across the alley, there were several pink underthings flapping around.

"Ladies underwear right there!"

Shanghainese were truly reprehensible. What could he do? Let the wind blow ladies underwear right over onto Yue Fei's Face?

He closed his eyes and dropped his face.

"To look at them is an offence... It's just too much: Ladies underwear just hung just..."

But he had some kind of problem: As if drawn by a lead, Shi Zhaochang simply couldn't forget those little pink panties. He glanced around without moving his head at all.

Couldn't see them.

What if Guan Yu could see them? Guan Yu's eyesight is keen: he has phoenix eyes!

What was he doing putting this on Guan Yu, damnit!

Shi Zhaochang hesitated three minutes before moving his head to sneak a look. He immediately looked at Yue Fei, as if in fear that he would know. But Yue Fei just kept puffing out his belly and didn't pay any attention.

He suddenly thought of that Woman Warrior of National Salvation: did she wear a pair like that...

He forced his mind to focus. That kind of useless thinking could easily lead to disaster. He closed his eyes and tried to remember the moment before the woman warrior had left: Smiling like this, bending like this, lifting her hand like this—and a flying shot!

Someone's gongfu was better than his.

He placed his hands behind his back and began to pace with his head bent down so he was looking at his feet. He really wanted to tell Brother Hu Genbao about the Woman Warrior. Soon he was grumbling that the Supreme Ultimate Master still hadn't arrived. He had to learn quickly so that he could demonstrate some skill to his Thirteenth Sister. Then they could go off together to do great things.

He sighed.

"It must be quickly."

But for now, he had to do his daily exercises lest he lose those boxing techniques. At eight in the evening he would add another few patterns to his exercise.

He took off his mouse-grey gown and threw it on the bed and then stood reverently. A breeze came in from the window and his body broke out in goose-pimples. His eyes were pointed directly at the balcony over there. But he couldn't see clearly if the pink shorts were hanging there or not.

Suddenly—he crouched down in a squat, arched his back as much as he could, like a monkey. His eyes seemed to burn with fury. He stretched his foot forward then pulled his hand out into open space to follow. In this way step by step he crouched his way to the window and then turned around.

After going back and forth ten-or-so times, Shi Zhaochang rubbed his legs.

"Ah, a little softer."—Those who study internal gongfu demand their muscles be soft.

Next he took out a few sets of metal rings from a basket and put them on his arms and desperately started to describe lines in the air.

The long hand on the desk clock was pointing at the "X."

He faced a pillar set into the wall and began his attack: he struck with the backs of his hand, struck with his fingers, his fists, his palms—Pai! Dong! Pi!

Only when the clock with its heavy sound struck nine did Shi Zhaochang pull back. The backs of his hands were reddened as if he had put on rouge. There was some white spots too. Every finger ached like they had been cut open.

He rubbed his hands, smiling.

"That's nothing. Doesn't hurt at all." He said to himself.

Then he switched his breathing—His stomach puffed out, then sunk in: Those who practice internal gongfu naturally don't breathe using their lungs. But it was uncommonly hard to take. It seemed like suffocation from covering someone's nose and mouth. His eyes rolled back in head several times.

Skilled people don't perhaps pant quite so much.

No. His cotton pants and jacket were so tight they made him pant.

He circled the room.

Downstairs the old women were yelling about something, interspersed with Shi Zhaowu's loud laughter. Suddenly a voice rose above:

"Madam! Look at Second Master!"

"Pai!"—The sound of a palm hitting flesh.

"Second Master hit me! Ai ya! What kind of behavior!"

"Haha haha!" The laughter became sharp and staccato. "Thigh! Haha haha! Haha!"

Shi Zhaochang furrowed his brow, but with a supreme effort, calmed himself down. He spread out his leather gown, sat cross-legged on the bed, and closed his eyes.

The shout of Little Wang, the cook, reached him from downstairs: "Second Master, how could you…"

The meditating man carefully said to himself, "I didn't

hear. I didn't hear."

He took in a lungful of air, but didn't let a bit of it out. Then he flexed his arm as much as he could. He opened his eyes halfway to look at it. He wanted so badly to test to see how much force his arm had. This was only elementary gongfu. It wouldn't be easy to train up to the skill level of someone like Gan Fengchi.

Little Wang's voice came up from downstairs again: "Second Master, what are you doing stealing my money! I'll tell Madam!"

"You wouldn't dare!"

"Give it back... Second Master, what are... you! I'm going upstairs to tell Madam!"

The sound of chaotic footsteps. It was probably Little Wang trying to get up the stairs to tell madam and Shi Zhaowu trying to block him.

"You wouldn't dare! If you take a step upstairs, I'll chop you into pieces!"

The swish of a cleaver.

The cook's sharp wild scream.

"Second Master is trying to kill me! Second Master!"

"I'll chop you into pieces!"

"Second Master!"

Someone ran off. It sounded like Shi Zhaowu.

Little Wang yelled upstairs, "A young master steals a chef's silver, and then came at me with a cleaver! Hmph! Master! I'll have my say on this. Should a cook be bullied by a young master? Dammit a young master stealing money, trying to murder, it's just..."

After this last, Shi Zhaozhang couldn't help but jump up. He rushed to the door and stood at the stairs. He pointed at Little Wang who was coming up the stairs and shouted,

"What did you say?! What did you say, you!"

The cook stood at the turn of the stairs with eyes wide open and left arm covered in blood: "Just now Second Master…"

"I know!" Shi Zhaochang stared him down, spitting the words at him. "If Second Master has gotten into trouble, then Master or Madam will give him a talking to. To have you say anything, you!"

"Did I say anything wrong?"

The Elder Mister Shi and Madam rushed down from the third floor. Liu Fu, the wet nurse, and the servants all thronged at the front of the stairs.

Shi Zhaowu pushed through the servants and stood in front of them.

Shi Zhaochang made a fist with his left hand and pointed at the cook with his right. "Second Master has Master and Madam to discipline him, what do we need you to say anything! Do you or do you not know your place, you! You do know what kind of person you are, you!"

"Second Master stole five dollars in notes: it was the money I asked to borrow from Madam last night. I wasn't… wasn't… Second Master cut me…"

"Shut your mouth!" Shi Zhaochang bellowed. He was so furious that he nearly passed out. "You know what you said: Where do you get the place to speak! Second Master is your master. What is a cook like you talking for! There must be order among people. Bastards who don't understand their place ought to be killed with a cleaver: That's why Second Master can take a cleaver to you!"

Shi Zhaowu applauded from down below: "Kill him! Kill him!"

The cook stared blankly for a moment. Then with a sobbing cry, "How? He steals my money and it's me who gets the chop!

You all live here and eat here at my place, I have to speak up about this, dammit, I…"

Shi Zhaochang charged down and put all his might into one blow: The cook tumbled down the stairs.

"People who don't know their place should be killed! I promise to cleanse the world of them—those bastards that don't know their betters! You all remember this: I will defeat any injustice, I must…"

Just then his stepmother interrupted him with her sharp voice, "Second Master has been a bit disruptive. Of course we'll take care of him. What are you—a cook—saying? It's not like you weren't aware of Second Master's temper. You should have put the money away safely. How can a person handle the pans and stove if he can't even handle his own money? It's infuriating! A person has a temper and you keep at him. Of course he's not going to get along with you—You don't even understand that! And here you are saying all this… all this.."

It seemed like she was trying to quote some classical phrase, but just couldn't remember it, so licking her lips she jumped into her next speech:

"When Second Master is sixteen, he will do out and do great things, leading soldiers and fighting the XX too, so now you should… You should that…"

A gust whipped in across her hair revealing her scar and she immediately gathered the hair back to cover it up, but only to have it blown away again.

"It's so maddening!" She muttered, sticking out her right arm for The Elder Mister Shi to take and guide her back up to the second floor.

Little Wang had been grumbling the entire time.

"…I have to speak up about this, I have to speak up about

this: stole my money, chopped at me, and then called in other people, didn't he? I'm putting my life on the line…"

But Liu Fu pulled at him hard and made him leave.

"Listen to me!" Shi Zhaochang said to the old women who had raised their hands at the bottom of the stairs. "A person must know their place, know their betters. Those that don't are following the path of Evil. Evil must be killed and hacked at…"

Everyone was silent. There was only the sound of his voice in the entire building—echoing off the walls.

He felt that he should say something more, but he couldn't' think of anything else to say. To just shut up like that was a little too… He looked at them for a while, rubbing his hands together and trying his best to look like he couldn't care less, he walked upstairs.

"What a pity that Little Wang is lost on the evil path!"

He walked with a steady gait and sat by the table.

What really happened with Little Wang?

If he really had gone Evil, Little Wang must have a master— some evil monk or something like that. He might have all kinds of dark sorcery. But as soon as Good shows up, it won't have a chance.

For two hours, Shi Zhaochang leaned on the table. He pushed his hands at his temples so that his eyebrows and the corners of his eyes were lifted up. The eyebrows of martial arts heroes were always lifted up like that. Just like the *wusheng* in the operas, he planned to find success through work.

There was a sudden crash from the window.

What! He was startled. Who could be sure it wasn't Little Wang coming for revenge!

He stood up and lifted his hand to shade his eyes from the dazzling lamplight to look toward the window. Nothing was there.

"Hm. Wind."

But after having given Little Wang such a lesson, he would certainly come for revenge. And he had that evil master. The master and disciple would probably come to do him in: Evil and Good can never coexist.

Maybe it was cold or something else, but he shivered.

He wanted to close the window. But he couldn't be sure that Evil was lurking out there. His heart raced. His head felt swollen.

"Someone cast a spell on me!"

He retreated a step. His leg knocked over the chair that was behind him—Bam!

Come at me! He immediately leaped away landing facing the chair in a perfect horse stance with his hands in a ready position.

The chair laid there motionless.

"Hehe. The sorcerer must fear my Goodness!" Shi Zhaochang laughed. "I have no fear of your tactics!"

He stood up. His legs trembled slightly. If the sorcerer had used a secret flying blade…

In the books, they say "A spear thrust is easy to evade in the light; an arrow in the dark is hard to defend against." Moreover, Shi Zhaochang's gongfu wasn't very profound. If the master and disciple were to put one over on him, well, there is a phrase for that too: "mortal peril."

But Shi Zhaochang pulled all his strength together and laughed toward the window: "I'll let you go this time!"

The words echoed back to him. Then suddenly the bamboo poles on someone's balcony—Crack! And then the shutters slammed shut with a crash. And that was nothing. The shutters opened right up again, and they weren't open for more than a few seconds before slamming shut again. And it went on slamming open, slamming closed. Open, close.

Shi Zhaochang leapt to the bed. A chill went through his entire body, and every hair stood up straight. His heart was pounding fit to burst.

What could he do! He looked at Yue Fei: Yue Fei just puffed out his belly again, paying no attention to this struggle. Was he, Shi Zhaochang to end like this? Sent to his death by the evil master and his disciple for nothing?

He recalled that filth can be used to counter evil sorcery, but there was no chamber pot in his room. There wasn't one in the entire house. There was only the flush toilet in the bathroom—flushed clean with not even a drop of urine in it. This was all the fault of the damn foreigners. They didn't know anything: not even the usefulness of filth.

"Dammit!"

There was one thing more effective than filth at countering evil sorcery: women's underwear. But he didn't have any. Men's underwear was clean, so it was useless. Where could he get some? He remembered the pink shorts from the other balcony, and that reminded him of the Woman Warrior. If the Woman Warrior could give him a pair… But of course she wouldn't: They weren't on those kind of terms yet.

Then in a flash of insight, he remembered another thing that was equally effective. He picked up a copy of the Daoist scripture *The Tract of the Most Exalted on Action and Response*.

He worried about someone coming up behind him, so he put his back against the wall. His face was drained of color, and he panted out his breath. His hands, dripping with sweat, gripped the book.

The electric light swung and so his shadow wavered back and forth. He didn't dare even look at it.

He was not resigned to dying like this. He still had his great enterprise. He hoped that in this moment of extreme danger, Brother Hu Genbao would appear to save him. The Woman Warrior of National Salvation would come too, shooting her missiles at the sorcerer. It was the Will of Heaven that he, Shi Zhaochang would save the people of the world. He could not die. Perhaps at that very moment, the Supreme Ultimate Master was sitting on some mountaintop having a sudden premonition, and just like that is calling Hu Genbao to come and bring their arts to bear against the sorcerer.

He stood like that for twenty minutes or so. He didn't move a muscle. He breathed out, "hmph. In the end he doesn't dare come closer!"

It sounded like something from a book. Judge Bao didn't have any magic, but he was an upright man. Sorcerers feared him.

Shi Zhaochang left his wall and lifted up that chair that had fallen. With all his effort, he forced an unconcerned façade.

But he still couldn't stop worrying about what Little Wang had suffered, that couldn't amount to nothing. In the life of a great hero, there were always a few setbacks, perhaps he, Shi Zhaochang this evening might…

Ah, he still needed to look into the disturbance.

He opened up a small leather case and pulled out a package—on the package were written two words: "Stealth Suit." He then cautiously opened the package, picked up the stealth suit in his hand and gave it a look over.

The stealth suit was a deep blue color. The pants and top were connected in one piece. Around the waist were three red stripes. Inside on the upper part were two foreign numbers in yellow: "36." At the collar on a square of white cloth was written:

Tianjin Heyi Company,
Extra-Fine Quality,
Special Swimming Suit,
$7.50.

He planned on putting the stealth suit on and going to check out the disturbance outside Little Wang's room. He took off his mouse-grey gown and put on the stealth suit. But the stealth suit wasn't big enough. He couldn't very well take off his padded-cotton shirt and pants: catching a cold was no laughing matter. He would just be patient and get into it.

No luck.

He was infuriated. A little more effort: RIP! A big seam tore open in the stealth suit.

"Dammit!" He threw the stealth suit onto the floor.

He didn't know if it was possible to go investigating the disturbance without the stealth suit. But one had to be patient and not go counter to custom: he wouldn't go down without the stealth suit.

Shi Zhaochang sat on his bed staring blankly, his fingers growing cold.

The clock on the table produced its measured tick tock, letting time go by second by second.

What was he staring for? Would the cook Little Wang really plot anything against him?

Dear readers, if you have read many gongfu novels, or seen many gongfu movies, you will know that whatever it is like outside of China, the luck of warriors is always excellent: when it comes to the critical juncture, they will meet with their savior. Here the author can provide a word: If you wish to know of the great warrior Shi Zhaochang's fate, "attend well to the elucidation of the following chapter." Then you, dear readers, may wait at ease.

However, our great warrior was not so at his ease. His legs were turning weak. He feared that Little Wang might have some plot. Dear readers, let us undertake a task for Shi Zhaochang: We will go to Little Wang's room and look into the disturbance. It is helpful that if we do not wear the stealth suit, we will not violate custom.

The 10 watt bulb in Little Wang's room gave off an orange glow.

The shadows of two figures stretched out on the wall. That is to say that aside from the cook Little Wang, there was another person sitting there. Was it that sorcerous master? It doesn't seem so. If he would lift his face up we would see he is familiar to us: Ah, it's Liu Fu. The cook was brooding.

"What can I do?" He voice quavered. "Do I just take it?"

"Don't lose your temper, buddy. If you lose your temper, you're the one who gets the worst of it."

"I can't take it…"

Liu Fu put a hand on Little Wang's back. "Don't be stupid. You just said that you wanted to go home. If you go home, is there anything to eat or drink? You don't know Shanghai that well. Don't think you'll be able to find work if you leave here."

Xiao Wang began to cry.

"What are you crying for?" Liu Fu said abruptly. "I've taken a lot worse than you. If I'd been like you I'd have died long ago… When you are eating the food of other, you have to be a little patient. Later on there'll be a chance to go your own way, but now if you don't control your temper, you'll be starving right quick! Think about it: your wife, your kids, they're all relying on you…"

At that he raised his head to look at Liu Fu.

Old Liu was sixty years older than he was, he had seen more of the world, and what he said made sense. To not control one's temper is to starve. There were five of six mouths waiting for Little Wang to bring home food and stuff it in them. He couldn't ignore that.

But would Master and Mistress still want him?

"But anyway… anyway…" he stuttered out.

"Anyway what?"

"They wouldn't…"

Old Liu understood, and scratched his head. "You're afraid they'll kick you out?"

All that answered him were Little Wang's still-moist eyes.

"I'll go talk to them for you." Lao Liu's brows lightly wrinkled. He told Little Wang to go to Master and Mistress early the next day and apologize and offer reparations. He'd also have to go over to the Young Master's place too.

The cook puffed out a sigh.

"Now, don't go thinking too much about it." Liu Fu patted him. "That's just the way it has to be. No doubt about it."

The way it has to be. The next day after breakfast, Little Wang and Liu Fu went to Shi Zhaochang's room.

Shi Zhaochang lept up.

"Bring it on! Ah!" He immediately prepared himself: his legs bent into a squat, palms stretched out ramrod straight, and he breathed in a bellyful of air.

Then just like that—the cook threw himself to the ground.

What? Without even one blow, the opponent falls? Only Gan Fengchi could pull that off. Surely he hadn't learned that gongfu without even knowing it?

He stared at his hands, then looked at the man who had fallen to the ground. His mouth gaped open.

Oh, Little Wang was kneeling to give a kowtow.

He must be careful! He remembered there was a man named Xu in ancient times—He knelt to kowtow and then shot out three hidden flying blades.

Shi Zhaochang spoke out very loudly, "If you want to fight, you must come and go in clear sight. No hero uses hidden blades!"

That cook, who had entered the path of Evil, replied in this way: "Master, yesterday evening I affronted you. Please Master…"

"What?"

"I beg of you Master to forget the events of yesterday evening. I was in the wrong. I beg of you…"

Shi Zhaochang slowly straightened his legs and put his hands on his hips. He arched his neck and gazed down on Little Wang.

"Ah, Ah," He said with a nasal tone. "As long as you know your offence is enough… Fine. Rise. I pardon you."

"Yes, yes. Thank you Master…"

The happiness swelled his head: To turn the cook from Evil to the path of Good was his accomplishment.

"Rise already, rise," He kept his face deliberately impassive.

"Let me ask you: Yesterday evening, you had entered onto the dark path, is that true?"

The other man did not understand, and could only open his eyes wide.

"The dark path. You understand? Yesterday evening, you must have entered onto the dark path?"

Little Wang stared for a while. "Uh-huh."

"And now I have subdued you. Do you submit?"

Another long stare. "Uh-huh."

"As long as you return to the Correct path, I will not blame you. You were ensorcelled yesterday evening. It was so bad that you didn't even know your own place, and I couldn't let that stand. Evil cannot triumph over Good: Of course not. I have subdued you... You must be careful to be good from now on, eh? Listen to my words. If you ever ensorcelled by Evil, you must come to me for help. Do you understand? Betters, inferiors, respectable and detestable, do you understand? The great and the petty... I must handle all those who enter onto the dark path: I will fight injustice anywhere under heaven... This...I swear my oath, if I do not do this, I'm no hero. If I don't, I'm nothing but a bastard..."

"Uh-huh!"

"Alright, alright."

But as Little Wang crossed out over the threshold, he called him back.

"Ah, I grant you two *mao* in cash. Go forth and let everyone know: For those that leave the dark path for the light, I will grant rewards. Go forth and let everyone know: True heroes care not for lucre. Spend it as they will, and without a thought. Go forth and let everyone know: I have rewarded you."

"Uh-huh."

As he watched Little Wang and Liu Fu leave, he felt like jumping up and down. This was his first step on the path of a warrior. Now he would have to just take things one by one as they come.

He had a "Guangdong Double Dime" in his hand: He had originally meant to give Little Wang four *mao*, but then thought that might be a bit much for an award, and so he kept that coin in his hand. He put his hand in his pocket and left the coin there. The clink made him remember that he had a lead dime in his pocket as well, and he regretted that he hadn't given Little Wang the lead one.

"Hmph. Didn't think about it at the time."

That was a regret.

Happiness is happiness, but there was a regret. But—

"There's nothing uncommon about spending two *mao*"

Shi Zhaochang tried to cover over that regret with words: "The warrior gives everything in fighting for righteousness."

That night, after practicing his gongfu, he told Lord Guan about this. He was worried that if he knelt on the ground he might get his pants dirty, so he knelt on the sofa.

"Oh hear me Lord Guan: I, Shi Zhaochang have completed an undertaking. I have subdued the cook Little Wang. I have caused him to move from the path of Evil to the path of Good. I also gave him two *mao*. And not the lead kind, either... I must completely fulfil the ambition that I have established. But I must have The Supreme Ultimate Master as my teacher. But I don't know if we are fated to be together. Please send me a dream, Lord Guan... Ah yes and there's The Woman Warrior of National Salvation..."

When he got into bed, he cast an eye at Yue Fei: He might be unhappy that he had talked to Grandfather Guan and not him, but Grandfather Yue would have been able to hear it too anyway.

He closed his eyes and waited for Lord Guan's dream: He dreamt of performing the wedding bow to heaven and earth with the Woman Warrior of National Salvation who was wearing pink panties. Elder brother Hu Genbao was matchmaker. Suddenly Little Wang came up with a double dime and exchanged it for a lead *mao* coin and then bought a ham as a gift for him.

He also dreamt of his stepmother taking a bath.

5

Paying Respects to
The Supreme Ultimate Master

O N SUNDAY MORNING, Shi Zhaochang and Hu Genbao were walking on the street. There was also another gentleman who you, dear readers, are not familiar with: not quite forty years of age, and a bald head with no hat. He had a sharp nose that stuck out like the beak of a parrot. His upper lip hung over his lower lip, and his chin wasted away to almost nothing. It was as if someone had rubbed his face from forehead down, and everything just grew downward. His upper eyelids stuck out three of four *zhang* from his face as if they were setting up awnings for his eyes. He was taller than Hu Genbao, and he had a larger face. It was no wonder that Hu Genbao called him Elder Brother Disciple.

As soon as Shi Zhaochang saw his Elder Brother he started to tell him the story of subduing the cook, but Big Brother didn't seem excited at all. He just pulled him outside for a walk while explaining who his Elder Brother Disciple was:

"This is my Elder Brother Disciple Half Mote."

Elder Brother Disciple started to chat with Shi Zhaochang with a thick Changsha accent, but every so often, he would throw out a few words in the "lower river" manner too.

"Elder Brother Disciple came to Shanghai…"

"I just got here." He looked up to see the shop signs. "I rode one of them fern ferries down from Hankou."

"Fern ferry?" Shi Zhaochang was taken aback.

"Yeah, Fern ferry. Them ferners' ferries."

Shi Zhaochang still didn't understand.

Elder Brother explained it to him: "Foreign Ferry."

"Oh."

"Fern ferries are them stem butts what run on the Yankee."

Hu Genbao told his second brother that the "Yankee" was the Yangtze, and then patted his left arm on his leg.

"Elder Brother Disciple was called to Shanghai by Master: Master had him come first."

"The Supreme Ultimate Master is coming?" Shi Zhaochang was struck.

"Oh, he'll be here very soon." Elder Brother looked very carefully at a dim sum restaurant. "It's hard to say if the Master hasn't already arrived. You just have to… have to… you have to be fated. Heaven calls on you… a great meeting… if it's fated you will meet The Supreme Ultimate Master."

Shi Zhaochang's heart beat wildly, but he worked to keep calm. He locked his eyes on the ground. He took care to measure his stride, and to not push out his chest with his breathing. He waited for Elder Brother Disciple to continue speaking, but his waiting was interrupted.

The sun crawled up from the southeast to the center of the sky. Shadows of all the different shops stretched out to the other side of the street like a half-collapsed wall—so untidy. A tram with a raised stick-like thing slid through the shadow.

Three or four XX soldiers were walking on the sidewalk. They swung their shoulders back and forth as if their shoes were so heavy that it made it tough to walk.

Shi Zhaochang's mouth curled down at the edges. "Idiots! Those riff-raff aren't worth anything. Just a casual touch on their pressure points, and they'd all be dead… And a little external gongfu would take care of eight out of ten of them."

One of the XX soldiers came up to them tilted his head to take a look. Shi Zhaochang's face flushed.

"They probably can't understand Chinese, right?" he asked himself.

Don't worry: the devils didn't understand.

Uh, he's not scary. All it would take would be an immortal swordsman with just a little training...

He started to talk with Elder Brother and Elder Brother Disciple about that. He felt the volunteer troops were useless, and perhaps those national salvation organizations were nothing but trouble too. All words he had gotten used to saying.

"There's only one way, and that's if we... but... but... Why doesn't Elder Brother Disciple go and... Why doesn't he..."

The stunned expression fixed its roaming eyes on Shi Zhaochang's face.

In this sober atmosphere, Shi Zhaochang felt that he had choked on the words in his mouth and couldn't spit them out. He wanted to ask Elder Brother Disciple: "If Master and Elder Brother Disciple have so much ability, why aren't they going out and killing the devils? He rolled the idea around on his tongue for a long while before the other understood what he meant.

His mouth open but silent, Elder Brother Disciple took a glance back at Hu Genbao.

Just then Hu Genbao's arm broke in between their shoulders followed by his whole body. He came to explain:

"Great things and small things are all Heaven's will. Master said that Heaven has already sent someone to kill the devils. There is no need for Master or myself to make a move."

Shi Zhaochang nearly jumped. He turned and faced Hu

Genbao and with a quivering voice, asked, "Who has heaven called to make this effort? Who?"

"I do not know." He said softly. "You would have to ask Master to know that."

Elder Brother Disciple was quietly reading a sign on a telegraph pole:

"Aid...help...vol...un...teer...troops...do...not...work... for...the...X...X...Every...body...fight...the...X...X...Im... per...i... ah...Lists. There's nothing after that. Whussat? "The XX Imperiah Lists?"

"It wasn't written by a scholar, of course." Shi Zhaochang furrowed his brow. "What do they know? Can you save the nation without studying? Ha! It must be so easy to save!"

Elder Brother Disciple read something else: "Nan...Jing... Res...tau...rant... I'm 'ungry...'"

"You're hungry?" Hu Genbao seemed a little unhappy.

"I only ate six of those muddon dumplins for breakfast. Then I walked from there to brother Shi's place. Walked so far, course I'm 'ungry."

Shi Zhaochang remembered then to ask where Elder Brother Disciple was staying.

"Jerkoff Road."* He answered. "In a friend's room. It's not too far from the Sunya Cantonese Restaurant. You know about the Sunya, right? The Sunya's right next to Jerkoff Road."

"Is it far from here to your place?"

"Real close—not far at all." Hu Genbao pushed hard at his back and he continued, "Ah, really far away."

They couldn't walk three abreast. The crowds of men and women pushed passed them on the sidewalk, so Hu Genbao fell behind them again. He looked nervously at Elder Brother

---

*   Half Mote is trying to pronounce Jukung Road.

Disciple. He wanted to push him back behind so he could walk next to Shi Zhaochang, but couldn't make it happen.

Shi Zhaochang wanted to talk to Elder Brother Disciple, but he was attracted to another sign.

"What's a 'National Salvation Thermos'?"

The other two were taken aback too, and they followed his eyes to the sign with pink characters.

Ah, underneath were some characters in black ink, and there were even some of those new Western punctuation marks too.

ONLY THE THERMOS CAN SAVE THE NATION!??!!!
The Northeast is bitterly cold. Therefore when the Volunteer Troops are making war against the XX. They often carry a Moonlight Thermos Set with them. Because Moonlight Thermoses are inexpensive but of exceptional quality. They stay warm for seventy-two hours. Patriotic Volunteers. Use in unending happiness. Therefore it is said:
ONLY THE THERMOS CAN SAVE THE NATION!??!!!
YOU CANNOT MISS THIS PATRIOTIC OPPORTUNITY!??

"There certainly are a lot of ways to save the nation." Hu Genbao mumbled to himself without any expression at all.

Shi Zhaochang grumbled, "What use are thermoses? If you have the Dao, you don't even have to drink water at all!"

No one responded. Elder Brother Disciple licked his lips and read from leaflets that were on a glass counter. There were drawings of snakes and chickens, and a dog-like something that wasn't quite a dog. "Dragon Phoenix Meeting," "Three Snakes Meeting," "National Salvation Vaudeville," "Masked Palm Civet Meeting," and the last one:

"*Bring out your conscience.*"

"What's that mean?"

Hu Genbao read them all from first to last and explained them to Elder Brother Disciple and Shi Zhaochang: These were all about big meetings, and you have to have a conscience to hold a meeting, so…

"This is a restaurant," Elder Brother Disciple interrupted loudly. "They should say, "Bring out your belly!"" He did his most to make the 'belly' come out in a strong lower river accent.

Shi Zhaochang pulled out cigarettes and offered them. Hu Genbao took a drag and spat out his new understanding:

"Ah, that's… They're afraid the customers won't pay, so they want them to 'bring out your conscience.'"

"Buying things without bringing money?" Shi Zhaochang glared, "This is injustice that must be righted!"

His clenched his hands into fists and looked behind him. He was still walking, but he bent his legs so that he could drop into a horse stance at any time.

"Trying to buy things without bringing money! What's become of this world, hmph! If you don't have money then you shouldn't buy anything! Back home there was one year when some common people came up to our house, they were wanting to buy without bringing any money—they wanted to buy rice. It was nothing less than burglary! Such impudence—one of them actually…"

Elder Brother suddenly struck Shi Zhaochang with all his might: "Master has come!"

Shi Zhaochang was so excited he couldn't stand still—But perhaps it was Elder Brother's blow that made him unstable, I'm not entirely sure. In any case, all his blood flew as quickly as electricity through his body, his heart was jumping enough to break his lungs apart. It's hard to express in words that kind of energy. Lovers separated for sixty years suddenly running into each other might have that sort of energy.

He followed Elder Brother Disciple and Elder Brother with a quick step. He eyes were peeled wide, searching everyone on the sidewalk. A living immortal will look different than ordinary people, he would know at a glance. But then a flood of people were coming out from the Isis Theatre and for a moment he couldn't see anyone.

Elder Brother Disciple and Elder Brother had gone up to someone and greeted him with respectful raised clasped hands.

An introduction…

No. No introduction. With one look, The Supreme Ultimate Master knew Shi Zhaochang and his history.

"Ah, it is Shi Zhaochang, come from the north."

His accent sounded a bit like he was from Hunan. Perhaps he was from Chenzhou.

Shi Zhaochang decided to kneel down and kowtow, but it wasn't easy on the concrete sidewalk. Just look at the ground: There's a big pile of lemon-yellow snot. To kneel there would certainly lead to dirty clothes. So he put his arms together and made deep salute from his nose to his heels, before bringing his hands back. Then a second salute. Then a third. Then he stood ramrod straight, with his head bowed and his eyes locked on his own nose to the point he was cross-eyed.

He wanted to say something to The Supreme Ultimate Master, but he felt his tongue stiffen up.

The Supreme Ultimate Master chuckled with Elder Brother Disciple. "So this is the disciple from the north."

This disciple from the north was doing all he could to keep

breathing.

"I suppose it is," said Elder Brother Hu Genbao.

"Eh…" The Supreme Ultimate Master jutted his chin out a bit. "Lift up your head and let me look at you."

Shi Zhaochang's forced his eyes away from the bridge of his nose to stare at the feet of The Supreme Ultimate Master. From there he went slowly upward. He first saw a pair of cotton-soled shoes, and yellow wool socks. Above this were two thin legs with satin bindings. Only a small stretch of the legs were visible: they were mostly covered by a deep grey gown. Moving further upward, there were five or six spots of grease to be discovered on the gown—very regularly spaced. Then the *magua* jacket, the lapels glistening with oil. Following on that, the shoulders and neck were unseen, because next appeared the chin…

Shoulders and neck?

You would see the ear before seeing any shoulder. His shoulders were so high that his neck, so short to begin with, was shortened to nothingness.

His tiny head was nearly buried between those two shoulders.

Then he looked upon the visage of The Supreme Ultimate Master.

There was a beard: Only a few wisps from nearby the two corners of his mouth, everywhere else was hairless. His eyes were red, only a dull red compared to the rims of his eyes. And in the corner of his eyes hung moist rheum. His face was very sallow, with several areas running to the green. All this topped with a rather pointed head.

Shi Zhaochang couldn't tell how old he was. From looking at him he couldn't be more than forty, but of course that couldn't be true.

"He has potential, this boy!" The Supreme Ultimate Master smiled, showing off two gold teeth, and one tooth bordered in gold. "Do you know who you were in a previous life?"

"I don't."

"Of course you don't know. In your previous life, you were… you were… I'd better not say. The mysteries of heaven must not be divulged… I knew right when you arrived in Shanghai… Half Mote, you were just talking about me, weren't you?"

Elder Brother Disciple Half Mote nodded casually. Hu Genbao glanced at him and he quickly took a respectful posture and belted out: "Yes!"

"I had a sudden feeling that you were discussing me so I came from Hankou. I just arrived… There are so many people here, Motherfucker!"

Half Mote smiled broadly, and pulled at Shi Zhaochang's sleeve. "Let's go to Sunya and sit for a while. What do you think? We can talk a bit."

Shi Zhaochang wanted The Supreme Ultimate Master to show them a little bit of his skill, but he didn't dare ask. Those skills shouldn't be used lightly.

He hadn't even spoken to The Supreme Ultimate Master, only two words. No hurry. Once at the teahouse they could talk at their leisure. He needed to tell The Supreme Ultimate Master about the oath he made at the temple to Guan Yu and how he had given his life over to his mission. And the first step had already been taken: The cook had been turned from Evil to Good. He was fated: he was the disciple that The Supreme Ultimate Master had spoken of!

"Should I mention the Woman Warrior of National Salvation?"

People who cultivate the Dao don't talk about women. The

Supreme Ultimate Master might tell him to not have any interaction with women.

The vision of the Woman Warrior of National Salvation kept floating up again.

He didn't believe that his relationship with the Woman Warrior was ended: The two of them still had some destiny together. They would save the nation together, righting injustice. Women Warriors were very rare.

Breathing shallowly, he looked at The Supreme Ultimate Master. The Supreme Ultimate Master was saying something to Elder Brother Hu Genbao with a belch.

"In the future, if you aid me well... Heaven will call on him..."

Shi Zhaochang set aside what he had been thinking and focused to hear if The Supreme Ultimate Master was talking about him.

Elder Brother Disciple looked both ways and pulled The Supreme Ultimate Master across the street. "To Sunya, to Sunya. Brother Shi will treat."

He was anxiously waiting for a car going south, and then for a tram going north.

The Supreme Ultimate Master wasn't even looking at the impatience in Elder Brother Disciple's face. He just kept casually talking to Hu Genbao. He belched so powerfully he had to put a hand to his mouth and try hard to keep himself together, his brows wrinkling as if in pain.

"He hasn't studied the Dao with me before, I should set out some of my feats of virtue... Feats of virtue, he should..."

"When I was in Hankou, he saved me," Hu Genbao leaned in close to The Supreme Ultimate Master's ear as he glanced back at Shi Zhaochang making it look like he wanted to talk privately, worried that someone might hear them. But his voice was so loud that no one could avoid hearing everything clearly.

"Yes," The Supreme Ultimate Master said matter-of-factly, "Ah, that's why I had you test him, to see if he actually is…"

Each and every one of these words penetrated Shi Zhaochang's ears. They were talking about him. But what? It was The Supreme Ultimate Master that sent Hu Genbao to test his heart? An inexpressible feeling rose in him: was it joy or disappointment?

But he really did have a deed of virtue: He had to tell The Supreme Ultimate Master about his Subjugation of the Cook. Right, he gave Little Wang two *mao*, too.

His hands were so sweaty. There were so many things he needed to tell The Supreme Ultimate Master: And there was the Woman Warrior of National Salvation, too.

Suddenly, it was like he had been struck hard.

"Thou shalt not get close to womanly charms…?"

The four of them planned to cross the street, but a truck came along and recklessly sprayed out water, soaking their shoes.

"Dammit!"

The Supreme Ultimate Master didn't quite know what was going on. He raised his bloodshot eyes to look for the truck, and another one came along right after it, towing a big leather-looking thing behind it to clean the streets.

He laughed. "Ah! Damn! What a huge washcloth!"

Elder Brother Disciple wiped his face, saying to himself, "They're all damn fern things."

"They've soaked my legs!"

"That's just not right."

Hu Genbao remembered fire-fighting hose being used to hose people down, and explained it in detail.

"They've had that in Beijing, too." Shi Zhaochang said guardedly. "It's to use against unrest. Upright people of course… But then maybe it wasn't Beijing. In any case, upright people wouldn't cause unrest. Upright people would…"

He looked at The Supreme Ultimate Master and worried he had said something wrong.

Several passers-by were looking at them now. Shi Zhaochang felt proud. They were taking in the visage of The Supreme Ultimate Master.

They were thinking, "Who are these people? That one who is like an immortal must the master of the other three."

If he were to tell them: This is The Supreme Ultimate Master…

But Shi Zhaochang felt a trifle uneasy at this. He thought of the permed one who threw mud-pellets.

"Those who cultivate the Dao maintain a pure Yang Qi, pure Yang… The pure Yang of the ancestors…"

Ah! The pure Yang of the ancestors! The Three Ploys of White Lotus!

He caught his breath and followed them across the street, his mouth repeating, "Sunya, Cantonese…"

After going up the stairs, a broad belt had stopped the three of them. Elder Brother Disciple was commenting on a posted note.

"It says it like this, they're saying XX people can't come in to eat. XX people cause trouble, so they're saying they can't come to eat. XX people cause trouble…XX… That's the path of Evil. Chinese people have the path of Good, nothing to worry about… so… so…"

6

The Power of The Supreme
Ultimate Master

THE SUPREME ULTIMATE MASTER did not eat any dim sum.

"Myself, The Supreme Ultimate Master, has not partaken of anything from the smoke and fire of the human realm for over three hundred years, to say nothing of some Cantonese dim sum!"

He only drank tea. He spoke to Shi Zhaochang of several schools: Confucius, Laozi, Shakyamuni, they were all good'uns, all worthy of faith. And Christianity and Islam had their points too.

"There is just this one word: 'Dao': these five schools are all the proper Dao. So I, The Supreme Ultimate Master, now... I've very... there is a global civilization now, so the immortals of China are in contact with the foreign immortals. When the foreign immortals drink tea, they like to add a little jellied fruit. Now this is..."

With this, The Supreme Ultimate Master took the dish of hot sauce and mustard and dumped them all in the teapot. Then he mixed it together with a chopstick.

Shi Zhaochang worried this only interfered with his job of listening attentively, he had eaten very little. He just sat there on his butt staring at the face of The Supreme Ultimate Master. His back was hunched so much that his neck stuck out and he strained to breathe. He was always looking for an opportunity to tell his story about subduing cook Little Wang, but The Supreme Ultimate Master never closed his mouth. From talking about the foreign immortals, he started in on Liu Bowen. *

"Young Bowen lives up on Mount Kunlun now. He plays chess and drinks tea with Ji Dian the Mad Monk" **

Eyes locked on the teacup, he carefully poured a little from the pot. "Several of us friends have been planning to build a platform for refining immortality pills, and to ask for donations from disciples who have potential, to donate for this…"

"I could donate too, would that be alright?" Shi Zhaochang caught the eyes of The Supreme Ultimate Master.

He smiled like an adult praising a child. "Of course, you must donate. You have potential: In your previous life… Your previous life… Ah, these are the mysteries of heaven not to be revealed by man… In the future, your Elder Brother Disciple and Elder Brother both will aide you in your great task."

"Shi Zhaochang stared at his Elder Brother Disciple: He was chewing on something with great gusto, his cheeks puffed tight like rubber balls. Then he swallowed with a great echoing gulp while his eyes rolled back in his head. Then he picked up another great bun. He spat out bones impatiently, as if eating the bun were a job he was not very interested in doing. He muttered, "Aghmargh, uh, hruhruhruh, wu?"

---

* Liu Bowen, or Liu Ji, (1311–1375) was an advisor to the rebel leader who would overthrow the Mongol Yuan Dynasty and establish the ethnically Han Ming Dynasty.

** Ji Dian, Ji Gong, or Lord Ji (1130–1207) was a Song Dynasty Zen Buddhist monk known for unorthodox behavior and magical powers.

No one understood him. No one asked.

Elder Brother Hu Genbao looked at another table, his eyes glued to some women. Every so often, he would make a gesture implying that they were "old thresholds." Then he'd switch to Cantonese to call out to the tea server, "Fogai!"

The Supreme Ultimate Master swept his bloodshot gaze across the three faces, then looked back to his teacup. He spoke to the teacup, "You have native ability. I, The Supreme Ultimate Master, will certainly take you on as disciple. Have you performed any feats of virtue?"

Shi Zhaochang stared dumbly. Who was he asking? Was it? How could...

"Hm?" The Supreme Ultimate Master jerked his head up.

"Uh, uh, yes." The young man's head dipped several times. "I was... Lord Guan and...The Sacred Lord Guan... I already subdued..."

Those closed eyes: The moist rheum had all been squished out of the eye sockets. He heard Shi Zhaochang continue speaking. He replied with his nose alone, as if marking the beat to the story. His face held no expression as if the events of the story were nothing of any note. This made Shi Zhaochang more than a little uncomfortable. His eyes didn't leave that utterly unflappable face for a minute while he used all kinds of gestures to describe the events of that night—Those events are all known to you, dear reader. What a pity that I told you so early. Otherwise, what an outstanding piece of work I could write about his narration right now!

Shi Zhaochang went on as if he were reading from a gongfu novel.

But The Supreme Ultimate Master maintained impassive closed eyes: the muscles on his face hadn't even twitched. Shi Zhaochang wiped the sweat from his nose. His voice cracked higher. He shot a glance at Hu Genbao and Half Mote: they weren't listening. His voice rose higher again. He wished that The Supreme Ultimate Master's face would just tense up a little, or maybe if he could smile a bit.

"He didn't go to sleep, did he?"

No: All he had to do was wait a moment, and there was a perfectly peaceful: "Hm?"

So he took another breath and kept on with the story. He started to lose a little conviction about this master. He stared back in reprisal at those closed eyes of The Supreme Ultimate Master: And he suddenly noticed that The Supreme Ultimate Master's eyelids didn't have a single eyelash.

"Ah? He doesn't have eyelashes, ah!"

For some reason, this put him more at ease.

His voice went higher again reaching into a falsetto. This is how he told the climax of the story—

"I gave him two *mao*, two *mao*!—Cash!—not lead! Two *mao*!"

The Supreme Ultimate Master raised up his teacup and took a sip, and with a "wa!" he spat it to the ground.

The table of ladies next to them quickly moved their legs out of the way and leveled a glance at The Supreme Ultimate Master, then looked to their shoes, muttering a few choice words.

"I'm sorry, I'm sorry," The Supreme Ultimate Master cupped his hands toward the ladies.

Shi Zhaochang was taken aback: How could they be so disrespectful toward his master! And Master even cupped his hands to them—to women!

He lifted his butt an inch out of his chair, silently preparing... He stared out: His line of sight lit upon the body of one of the ladies.

The Woman Warrior of National Salvation!

He sat back down.

"Uh, no."

She looked a little like her.

"I still have too much fire *qi*," he said to himself. "Master doesn't have any fire *qi*."

He drank several mouthfuls of tea to settle himself. He had to finish telling his story and hear any admonitions that The Supreme Ultimate Master might have. He also had to tell him about The Woman Warrior of National Salvation. And then, he had to ask The Supreme Ultimate Master to select a propitious day to take him as disciple. Things must be arranged quickly, the devils had already driven into X Province!

But there was that old saying: As long as something is arranged by heaven, everything will proceed smoothly. It goes without saying that Shi Zhaochang would be taken as disciple by The Supreme Ultimate Master. He would need a Thirteenth Sister too, that wouldn't stand in the way of cultivating the Dao.

"You are still very young. Of course, you will have to find a Woman Warrior."

The Supreme Ultimate Master, eyes still closed, spoke of the date: When the date came, they would hold the ceremony to take him in as disciple. They would need to invite guests. After that he could teach him some Daoist skills.

"Like blade-spitting, like the Passing Through the Five Elements?"

For a disciple with native ability it is easy to learn those. The Supreme Ultimate Master was calculating a date.

"Um, they could be learned in a week or two."

"Not even a fortnight," Shi Zhaochang said, sounding it out. He looked at Elder Brother and Elder Brother Disciple.

"After a fortnight, I...I...I could, for example, I could manage those...those..."

"Sure, a fortnight," The Supreme Ultimate Master lifts his teacup, but then remembered the taste of the tea and quickly put it back down.

Shi Zhaochang nearly fainted. It was shocking; he was so happy.

"A fortnight... a fortnight... Dammit, ah! So simple!"

Not only that, but Elder Brother Disciple was inviting everyone to where he was living.

"Come to my place...It's not so far: not more than six blocks. Come to my place and we'll eat. Whoever wants to treat us to dinner can do it at my place." He looked with a little fear at Hu Genbao at that. "Well, my place is actually pretty far away: I'm not even sure how far away it is... Who's treating?"

"I'll treat," Shi Zhaochang patted his belly. He needed to be a generous as possible now.

Elder Brother Hu Genbao left abruptly, making a gesture for them to wait.

"We'll all help you," Elder Brother Disciple Half Mote put his right hand on Shi Zhaochang's shoulder. "Master told us to help you with your veats of fertue You'll treat today, but Master is a living immortal, so he doesn't eat. He's..."

"I can eat a little," The living immortal interrupted. His reasoning was this: He had never met a disciple with such a background as Shi Zhaochang had. Looking at his face, he would make a bit of a sacrifice. But—"But, I've never done this before. Next time—This shall not be a precedent."

Shi Zhaochang saluted him with his two trembling clasped hands.

The three stood and waited for Hu Genbao to return.

Half Mote grumbled, "What the... Old Hu still ain't back. How long's it take to call a cab?"

Shi Zhaochang was arguing with one of the servers: He was paying the check but the server said one of his coins was lead, and asked him to replace it.

"What? Your old man is cheating you with a lead coin? Your old man is benevolent with largesse! Why would I begrudge you two *mao*? Replacing it is nothing to me, but you can't say that I, Mr. Shi, am a cheat. Humph. Take it!"

He looked at everyone, and with a red face walked to the window, forcing himself to look out at the street as if nothing had happened. A XX woman walked past the entrance to the Isis Theatre.

"Don't let it get to you. In a fortnight... Hmph. Just you wait! And that server is a bastard!"

After half a minute, Hu Genbao called for them to come downstairs and get in the cab he had called. But The Supreme Ultimate Master wouldn't budge. He had something to take care of and would go to Half Mote's place in in a while.

The driver got the three of them settled in the car and then looked back at them and couldn't stifle a chuckle: "These three stiffs—going for a tour in this cold, they'll catch their death!"

With that he started off southward on North Sichuan Road.

Not very far, right?" Shi Zhaochang asked.

"Oh it's far!"

It was truly far. Shi Zhaochang felt that the car must be going very fast, but it was a very long ride. He looked out the window: the streets flew by. The car turned east at the post office, then the road twisted to the south and over a large steel bridge. Steamboat piers. And he also saw a copper bodhisattva. Then they turned west: This road he recognized.

"Isn't this Avenue Edward VII?"

They kept going west. Damnit this road was long. Eventually they turned north. And then after a while, they turned east.

"Here's the horse track," Elder Brother Disciple pointed out on the right.

Then they made another turn at the New World Mall: to the north again. Always to the north. Then back to the east. Then back north. Over another steel bridge. Ahead—the road ended, so they had to turn east. Shi Zhaochang saw what he recognized must be a railway station. Then they turned north to Baoshan Road. After a while, they turned east, and Shi Zhaochang caught sight of a sign: "Jukung Road"

"We're nearly there, surely?"

"Uh-huh."

The roads weren't that smooth and the car's rumbling was enough to turn legs numb. The car went east, block after block.

Suddenly Elder Brother Hu Genbao called out: "We're here, we're here!"

Shi Zhaochang blew out a breath. "It really was quite far. It must be sixty or seventy li from the Sunya."

"Yeah," Elder Brother Disciple said as he led Shi Zhaochang upstairs. "And the car was fast. It was only an hour or so... If we had walked... Eh, even if we'd taken a rickshaw it would have been three hours... Old Hu is downstairs paying the cab. He'll be right up."

"Upstairs?"

"Yeah, upstairs. Step carefully here: pitch dark. This is my place."

Elder Brother Disciple Half Mote took out a key to open the door.

Shi Zhaochang was the first through the door. As soon as he looked in the room he was stunned. What? How!

There was a person sitting in the room chuckling at him.

Who was this person? Take a guess, dear readers.

Ah! The Supreme Ultimate Master! Absolutely, The Supreme Ultimate Master.

It was so far, they were speeding in a car for so long, but The Supreme Ultimate Master arrived first.

Then, as if it were entirely instinctual, his knees bent and he knelt: He kowtowed twenty-four times to The Supreme Ultimate Master. Right then he had seen the power of The Supreme Ultimate Master with his own eyes. But The Supreme Ultimate Master said this kind of power was only the most pedestrian. And using that as a topic to begin with, he wipes his eyes with his sleeve.

"There is a global civilization now, Passing Through the Five Elements isn't enough anymore: For example, I just came from Sunya to here using a different type of Passing Skill. Passing through Asphalt. Do you see? You can use it to pass through asphalt. It is… do you see? It is…"

Half Mote busied himself going downstairs to order food. Hu Genbao poured tea. The Supreme Ultimate Master went on talking nonstop. By the time the food was served, he had come back around to the plan for building a platform for refining immortality pills on Mount Kulun, and he asked Shi Zhaochang to contribute some funds.

"It is all fated, a little more, a little less, that doesn't matter. Your Elder Brother Old Hu donated two thousand dollars. Your Elder Disciple Brother—that third-wheel—uh, Half Mote… half Mote donated three thousand… These dishes are wonderful. If it weren't for the sake of Disciple Shi here I wouldn't eat, otherwise…"

The Supreme Ultimate Master has a great capacity for food and drink, and he ate fast. With one look you could tell he hadn't partaken of anything from the smoke and fire of the worldly realm in three or four hundred years. While he ate, he praised the Cantonese cuisine. Half Mote had ordered the dishes to go from Sunya.

Perhaps because the room was so small, Shi Zhaochang wasn't breathing smoothly. He felt like he was floating in midair, like his belly was full of light air. After a fortnight... but he wouldn't continue thinking along those lines. To think about things too happy would lead to difficulties: he had had that experience before.

He needed to think about unfortunate things.

Ah, contributing to building a platform for refining immortality pills on Mount Kulun! That thought was like a medicinal plaster applied to his mind that he couldn't take off.

He took a look at Elder Brother and Elder Disciple Brother: they had contributed two and three thousand. And he would need to give money for the Master to take him as disciple too.

"Need to do better than some two thousand dollars."

But perhaps The Supreme Ultimate Master would mimic the policies of companies: a winter cut in prices.

"Damnit, what's the good of trying to be clever about money. A hero cares not for lucre."

Spending money has its own methods, to spend, one must do the accounting: That day when he bought the Woman Warrior of National Salvation's tickets, when he gave two *mao* to Little Wang, this was all spent with reason. If The Supreme Ultimate Master truly has incredible swordsmanship, it would be nothing to dump out his entire wallet: In a fortnight he could make back his capital, and on top of that...

The Supreme Ultimate Master's skills were truly extraordinary: That day after eating, he used his Art of Withdrawal to allow Hu Genbao to take Shi Zhaochang back. When they exited the door to Half Mote's place and walked east not more than ten steps, at the intersection, suddenly there appeared the Sunya.

"That's Master's Art of Withdrawal," Elder Brother shook his pointy face. "Second Brother, look: The Sunya, the Isis Theatre. With one Withdrawal, we went back this far. The Art of Withdrawal is an old skill of the Chinese people. Lots of people can do it. It's nothing special."

Elder Brother also wanted to tell Shi Zhaochang: the withdrawal at the front line in XX Province was the same Art, but they just don't say it publicly. It's just that...

"Let me flag you down a rickshaw, Second Brother... Rickshaw!"

Shi Zhaochang felt that he had been a little disrespectful to The Supreme Ultimate Master: What was he doing before by trying to be so clever about money? Spending like this, he couldn't avoid being thought to have more money than sense. He felt himself floating again. He blamed it on the rickshaw driver not running fast enough.

"Hey! Faster!"

He put his hands in his sleeves. But his hands were burning hot, so he pulled them out and put them on his thighs. His mouth was tightly closed. The corners of his mouth curved down as he looked at a banner pasted over the entrance of a XX Shop:

"Congratulations to our Troops in X Province"

Who cares if you take another ten X Provinces: You'll see. After a fortnight there won't be anything for you to be happy about. By then...

Should he first take back X, or fight through to XX? By the time Shi Zhaochang stepped into his house, he still hadn't decided.

"I should just ask Master to make that decision." He lowered his head as he walked through the hall.

There seemed to be a lot of people in the guest room. His mother-in-law was declaiming her education strategy for Shi Zhaowu in her shrill voice. Shi Zhaochang heard one sentence: "Next year he will go abroad…"

"Heh," Shi Zhaochang laughed coldly as he turned back to the guest room: He wanted to hear their discussion.

7

A Shortcut to National Salvation

IN THE GUEST ROOM, everyone was familiar. The only unknown person was the young guy in a jade-green necktie. According to the introduction he was Mr. Liu Liu's eldest son Liu Zhao.

"Is this brother Zhaochang?" Liu Zhao rubbed his hands together. "I've heard a lot about you."

Mistress Shi puffed out a breath in her dissatisfaction at being interrupted. Touching the hair at her temples to see if it was covering that purple scar, she gently invited everyone to enjoy the melon seeds.

"Please eat the seeds. These are authentic Suzhou rose-roasted pumpkin seeds. Master Liu has been to Suzhou, haven't you? People from Suzhou say eating seeds is very good for you. They take food very seriously in Suzhou: their make wonderful dim sum. Back in Beijing, I had a cook from Suzhou. He was really a wonder. He could even wiggle his ears—what fun! The children would laugh themselves to death. The children all loved him, and demand that he tell them stories. Children always love to hear stories. Their teacher would tell them stories. Before, at school, there just wasn't anyone to tell them stories. They would, ah, they were just overwhelmed with homework. It was very hard, they hardly had time to eat. You must have some of these seeds, they're Suzhou seeds, Mr. Liu, have some. Mrs. Liu, ah, don't be so polite. Don't be so polite, well, our teachers weren't polite at all, so very strict with the homework—it was so difficult back when we were students. Now those people who become teachers, ai, it's infuriating, what's it matter?... it's like..."

Others had begun talking about the art of eating melon seeds. Mr Liu Liu brushed the shells off his clothes while describing a man from Suzhou who could eat fifty seeds in one second.

"And the meat of the seed was still whole!"

"Shi Boxiang nodded: "Suzhou'ers can really eat seeds. It's an odd thing, no one from outside Suzhou can out-eat them."

Liu Zhao was waiting for an opportunity to speak, standing there rubbing his hands like he was planning to perform. But he only spoke one sentence: "That's the Ethnic Essence of Suzhou people."

"What?" Said Shi Zhaochang.

"Ethnic Essence, it's the same as a National Essence, or just Essence for short." The reply was clear, and he looked around at everyone. "Like, eating hot peppers, that's the Ethnic Essence of northerners. The ethnic essence of northerners is eating steamed bread."

He licked his lips and continued. "Every ethnic group has its Essence. The Ethnic Essence is defined as that inborn thing that people of the area have in common. The XX people's Ethnic Essence is the worst, the cruelest. That's why they've invaded us. Our Chinese Ethnic Essence is to love peace..."

Shi Zhaochang didn't quite agree with this, and vigorously gestured with his right hand. "This is at odds with the Path of Good and Path of Evil."

"Not necessarily," Liu Zhao said loudly, but his face showed a courteous smile. "This is the Ethnic Essence. Although our Ethnic Essence is to love peace, at the point of no other recourse, we will resist. Isn't everyone resisting the XX for national salvation?"

"Yes!" Mr. Liu Liu chimed in with his son. "And there are those on hunger strike for national salvation, even the elite families are in for national salvation. And they're even preparing to campaign against the barbarian. They've already set to raising funds."

But it was as if the son hadn't heard. With the next breath he went on with his speech. He told everyone that in the past the Chinese people had been on top of the world, too.

"The Yuan Dynasty, for example," he gestured with his right hand. "During the Yuan, they fought all the way to Europe! This is our... That's our—Ethnic Essence. The Xinhai Revolution to tear down the Manchu Qing Dynasty: Ethnic Essence. The Chinese Essence is truly great... It would be best if we could have it like in the Yuan Dynasty: Conquer every nation! First we must campaign against the barbarians!"

The speechmaker raised his fist, with glaring eyes staring at everyone's expressions.

Shi Zhaochang couldn't help but speak up: "We only have to wait a fortnight and then there'll be a way."

Everyone was startled: What? Only wait a fortnight?

Mistress Shi felt that a fortnight wasn't enough time. They would have to wait for next year.

"Next year Zhaowu will be sixteen," She stretched out her neck. "If only Zhaowu does not lose his drive it will all go well. That child, I understand him. Those teachers don't understand him at all. Like that Teacher Zhang back in Beijing. Hmph, can you imagine what he said? He said Zhaowu would need to be held back a year, said Zhaowu had no prospects. I honestly have no idea what he was on about. Right, Young Master Liu? Eh, Mrs. Liu, isn't that so? Can you tell me how Teacher Zhang got so muddled?"

"Where was he from?" Asked Young Master Liu quickly.

"Teacher Zhang?"

"Yeah."

"Shandong, I think."

"Then that's the Ethnic Essence of people from Shandong."

"Ah, that's right, he was from Sichuan."

"Well, that's the Ethnic Essence of people from Sichuan."

Mrs. Liu was nimbly cracking into the seeds with her teeth. She looked over at Mr. Liu Liu and smiled knowingly, then she examined everyone's faces to see if they were admiring their Young Master Liu.

A coal brick went into the stove and crackled with a Pop! Pop! to rival the sound of cracking seeds. Shi Zhaochang took out his handkerchief to wipe away his sweat. He wanted to sit in the seat by the window, farther away from the stove, but there was so much he had to say to Liu Zhao. He stared at that jade-green tie across from him, waiting for someone else to question him. Everyone else forgot all about it. So he had to take it upon himself and ask:

"After a fortnight, there will be something new in play in China. You'd better believe it!"

"Based on what?"

Mr. Liu Liu explained for Shi Zhaochang with an odd confidence:

"That's to say that the "Campaign Against the Barbarians Fund" has been very successful, and after a fortnight, they can go on campaign, isn't that so?"

But Shi Zhaochang didn't know anything about any "Campaign Against the Barbarians Fund." It was just another kind of national salvation scheme. Even though he had heard Mr. Liu Liu explain it, his mouth stuttered out: It's useless!

Mr. Liu Liu paid no attention whatsoever to what anyone

else thought, he just snatched out a sheaf of documents and started spraying spittle:

"To campaign against the barbarians, there is of course the need for funding, and to have that funding relies on everyone's contributing. This Campaign Against the Barbarians Fund Committee of ours is especially formed to take care of that; this is a patriotic organization! It hasn't been long since we formed now, but we've already collected nearly ten thousand in contributions. The overseas Chinese in Southeast Asia can contribute some five or six hundred thousand, and overseas Chinese from elsewhere all together can contribute one or two million. Truly in only a fortnight, my son, one fortnight would be very impressive... The comrades of the Campaign Against the Barbarians Fund Committee are each and every one a patriot, and I am one of the committee members. The Hunger Strike for National Salvation is passive, but the Campaign Against the Barbarians Fund is active. We should come at this from both angles: passive and active. The XX must be obliterated... Like our Mr. Ren here." At this he pointed at an elderly man. "He is a secretary, Secretary Ren, but he was willing to resign his post and come to our committee and serve as a seventh-grade worker. Now that kind of patriotism is... it's so... So the Campaign against the Barbarian movement is so very important. My son is a member of the Campaign Against the Barbarians Fund Committee too: He is a third-grade clerk in the Communications Branch of the Office of General Services."

His son nodded. "The campaign against the barbarians is truly incredibly important. Compatriots from the entire nation want to unite. We can no longer have me fighting you and you fighting me. Individuals fighting will certainly be destroyed, isn't that so Shi Zhaochang? For example, workers should sacrifice a bit and work hard, if they start fighting on their own it'll be disaster."

"Hm," Shi Zhaochang nodded. "but those low-class people don't understand any of that. All they care about is scraping together a few coins. They don't care anything for patriots or traitors. And if you give too little money, they'll go on fucking strike!"

Young Master Liu patted at his clothes and rubbed his hands, earnestly trying to take Shi Zhaochang as a partner in the conversation.

"They are ignorant. They only care about themselves. An individual's hunger and poverty is really insignificant when compared to the national crisis, but still they don't understand!" At this, Liu Zhao shook his head. "What does starvation matter! Starvation doesn't amount to anything. And if it's a few ignoramuses that starve to death then that's even less important. Beyond that... beyond that... If the starved are... We have the Hunger Strike for National Salvation... As for the industrialists, well we can't have them starve—there are too few industrialists. Their exhausting toil has to be rewarded. And anyway, they use their very own money, there is no fault in them. So to move forward with strength in production is, you know... Critically... Without patriotism as a foregone conclusion you'll just stir up trouble: In action, there before one can... there must be a forgone..."

Mistress Shi had been listening intently, chewing seeds and nodding her head all the while. Here she broke in:

"Yes! Forehooves are the most important part: If you bring your horse into a gallop without surefooted foorehoves, you'll fall for sure. When we were back in the schoolhouse in history class, I recall the foorehoves being most important. When Lord Guan fought at Changsha, Huang Zhong lost the battle because his horse lost its footing, but that was fated by heaven. Fate is truly powerful, it says something will happen to you and that will happen to you. Fate tells us Zhaowu will go to lead soldiers next year, and what can we do about it? Ah, it's so pitiable, leading soldiers at sixteen, that child! It's pitiable these past few days he's been going on and on about patriotism. I tell him, "it's still early yet, if you want to love your country, you can wait until next year to love it! Your father has joined the Hunger Strikers for National Salvation, he loves his country three times a day!" But him! Oh that child! It just kills me, you know what he's like Mrs. Liu, haha haha. Oh, him! Sometimes at night he'll love his country by himself, or he'll go and get Liu Fu's…"

She started to laugh again, holding her sides and unable to go on. The way she laughed didn't really fit with her speech which sounded like a memorized script, so everyone just stared at her.

She laughed for over two minutes. Having laughed enough she looked up and was going to continue to talk, but the group had whisked Young Master Liu away. She muttered, "it just kills me," and opened up the stove to look at the fire, then called to have more coal brought in.

"Mother Yang, there's no coal in the guest room! Bring coal! So annoying, these old servants are so stubborn. If you don't scream at them, they'll never move a muscle. We have to have coal to burn, and the people in the house are all… are all…"

Liu Zhao had got to talking about the XX: They had a lot of people opposing their government's deployment of troops, and moreover…

"And we have to destroy XX imperialism."

"What kind of disease is that?"

Young Master Liu looked around and lowered his voice as if he were worried to let out a secret: "That's those unruly people. That's their Ethnic Essence."

Everyone stared, thinking: should that make me happy or worried?

"They'll destroy the nation, that's it."

Shi Boxiang pulled out that square-folded handkerchief to wipe his mouth. "Ah, XX slaves will soon... soon they will..."

"Not necessarily!" Liu Zhao eyes bulged. He said that if those unruly people from elsewhere took power, it would be a disaster too. "Disastrous, so disastrous. No matter which one takes over, it's quite dangerous to us."

"A big earthquake would be best, take those islands of theirs—there's three of them, right? Was it three islands or four?"

"That sort of thing is certain to happen: A big earthquake to come and shake their country to the ground—"The mesh of Heaven's net is large; but it lets nothing escape. * ""

Everyone seemed to relax, and reached out to the dish to take more rose-roasted pumpkin seeds.

But Shi Zhaochang felt his energy sapped: If the devils were wiped out in an earthquake without even one blade being spat, then who would get the credit?

"Ah, nothing so good would happen!" He said, slightly deflated. "They started all this on their own, that's how the Path of Evil fights the Path of Evil. We have to use the Path of Good to subdue them. In a fortnight, there will be someone who will make a move, you'd better believe it!"

"That's exactly the Campaign Against the Barbarians!" Mr. Liu Liu cried out. "Only by putting our all into raising

---

* Dao De Jing 73 (tr adapted from Legge).

contributions to campaign against the barbarians will we have another fortnight. This is the shortcut to national salvation."

Only with the utmost effort was Shi Zhaochang able to keep from shouting out what made him so painfully happy:

"Just you watch: Will it be you campaigning against the barbarian or me!"

His shortcut to national salvation was absolutely unambiguous. We couldn't hold in his enthusiasm, and like a shot he jumped up.

"There is another shortcut to national salvation."

"Another?"

"Oh. That's… That's…That's…"

8

In Love, Forget Not the Path of Good

"WHY DINTCHA COME to my place? I toldja to come! Tonight's the *Woman Warrior of National Salvation!*""

"Uh, I don't know the way."

"Why didn't ya just call a rickshaw then? Today you kin come over to my place… my house and eat, whadya think? I'll eat with ya!"

And who is this speaking a mouthful of perfect Mandarin Chinese?

The Woman Warrior of National Salvation, Miss He, He Manli—Mary Ho!

The man is our great warrior, Mr. Shi Zhaochang. Miss He had come to Shi Zhaochang's home and dragged him off, hailing a couple of rickshaws to take them back to where she lived.

They sat next to each other. There were men and women coming and going in the room. Their faces looked more or less the same to Shi Zhaochang. The men all wore suits that started coming out in the first year of the revolution,* some of them even carried those foreign guitars. The women were showing a good deal of leg, with heavily powered faces,

---

* Western suits rather than Chinese gowns.

running back and forth belting out:

"The deep chill is such a joy! The deep chill is such a joy!"

There were a few men playing music in the lower-floor guest room and the women were warming up their voices. While Miss He was chatting with Shi Zhaochang, she would occasionally shout out, "Wrong! You have to wait half a beat!"

Shi Zhaochang didn't know what to do, his whole body was trembling. Even his tongue was trembling. Whenever he spoke, he stuttered.

The Woman Warrior of National Salvation held a lit cigarette. She only puffed at it once or twice before stuffing it in Shi Zhaochang's mouth. He started, afraid that she was displaying more of her gongfu, but: so very soft.

He took a drag and looked at the paintings on the wall. They were all of foreign women, three quarters were nearly flashing their butts and the other quarter were—Ah, wearing stealth suits!

"Those women, those... Those are all Women Warriors? Foreign, right?"

She barely took a glance at them.

"Sure!"

"So many... So many..."

Suddenly she sat down on his lap. Suddenly her right hand hooked around his neck. She faced him: there was only an inch between their faces. As she opened up those painted-red lips to speak to him, a scent of sandalwood competed in his nose with a scent of something like dead rat.

"You got a lover?"

"What?"

"Do you have a girl that... that loves ya, that's it. You're..."

"I certainly don't... I certainly don't..." He sputtered a long while. He tried to tell Miss He about looking for a Woman

Warrior with whom he could do good deeds.

"Well, ain't I a Woman Warrior of National Salvation? We've gotta save the nation!"

Her meaning was perfectly clear: She was that Woman Warrior. He must go with her. The disaster was that he couldn't come up with a single sentence to say. His locked-up mouth just wouldn't work. He looked at her face, looked and looked until one sentence burst out:

"How old are you?"

What a shock: She hadn't had anyone ask her age since she'd been a kid. What proper person would ask her age?

But she just laughed.

"Why don't you take a guess?"

He couldn't guess. Her face was coated in powder. There were faint traces of freckles, like stars under clouds. There were wrinkles at the corner of her eyes. To look right at her, she looked about forty. From the side, about thirty or so. From the back? Nineteen. Shi Zhaochang made a guess, while taking a drag on the cigarette.

"Thirty-two? Twenty? Forty-nine?"

"None of 'em!" She said happily. "Lemme ask you: You like em young or old?

"Ought to be young... young...Eh. Well, how old are you?"

"Fifteen!"

"What!" He was stunned. He looked carefully at her, but found no reason not to believe. "But I... I... You are... I would say a little older would be better..."

Her laugh came out:

"I tricked you! I'm not fifteen. I'm... I'm forty."

"Forty?" Shi Zhaochang looked at her. He found no reason not to believe.

Miss He kept smiling, and looked him in the eye.

"The Modern Patriotic Song and Dance Troupe would like for you to make a donation."

"How much?" His voice quavered.

"Whatever you like: a hundred silver, two hundred, a thousand, whatever, it's all..."

He stared for a while, then pulled out his wallet. First he took out three hundred in silver.

"The rest I can get you next time..."

The woman shrewdly took the bills and counted them, then took them to look each one under better lighting before stashing them in her clothes. Then she calmly closed her eyes, arranging herself like lead in the movie *Doctor of Romance*, so that the male lead's lips could descend right on hers.

Shi Zhaochang was panicking. He didn't know how to approach this. He didn't really understand the rules of love. He tried to figure out if he should embrace her or kiss those lips. But was it allowed or not?

The books he read hadn't covered this. Was Thirteenth Sister so energetic? There was that other book, *Something Destiny*? It had romance in it: There was that rich scion who had spent so much money, and so women loved him. Shi Zhaochang had already done that part. But what that book didn't say—if Thirteenth Sister from Tianqiao had sat down on that scion's lap and closed her eyes. How should he handle it? It didn't say. Oh!

Miss He waited forever with eyes closed for any activity at all.

"He dunt git it," she thought. Such flowing Mandarin Chinese came from her mouth, and she used that Mandarin in thinking too.

She then thought she remembered in movies, there seemed to be a rule for women kissing men: Yeah! There was a rule for it! So with a pouting noise, she charged up to kiss him and whacked him hard enough to draw blood from his teeth.

"Ah! What gongfu!" the man said to himself.

Four lips came together as one. From the woman's side came a tongue, but the man's gongfu showed itself too—his mouth closed so tight as to not let it in.

In movies when they show a kiss, it always fades out, fades out, and shifts to another scene. Let us do the same and switch to a new locale.

The stage: curtain not yet raised. Next to the stage is a sign reading, "The Modern Patriotic Song and Dance Troupe Performance Schedule." The wall is covered with multicolored pasted bills: "Long Live National Salvation Song and Dance," "Only Song and Dance Can Resist the XX," "Patriots Should Come See Patriotic Song and Dance," "Support Patriotic Art," and "Patriotic Song and Dance Can Wipe Away National Shame."

The seats in front were packed with men and women. They clapped and whistled and laughed loudly.

Shi Zhaochang certainly wasn't there. Shi Zhaochang was in the backstage dressing room. The Woman Warrior of National Salvation Miss He Manli was introducing an artist to him.

"This is a great man of patriotic music, Mr. Hui. He plays the pee-yah-no like a fever in China, he plays so good! He's written a lotta songs too. Tonight in our patriotic song and dance, we're havin him play pee-yah-no—DONG dah DONG, DONG dah DONG! Pos-i-lute-ly wonderful!"

But the great man of patriotic music was edgy:

"How come the Grass-Skirt Burlesque has to use *La Marseillaise* and that other one... *Un Deux... Un Deux ...* That song has a key change in the middle, so annoying... I could never memorize those songs."

"That one... That one..." Miss He was trying to remember the foreign name for that song. "That Un Deux... *Un Deux Trois*... trois... We've got sheet music for that one."

"What good is sheet music—That's five-lined staff! I can't tell heads or tails with five-lined staff sheet music!"

"Well write it out in numbered notation real quick."

"How could I do that?"

The Woman Warrior of National Salvation thought a bit then cried out, "Hey! Ah Li! You can read five-lined notation, write this song out in numbered. It's a patriotic act! Help out Old Hui here."

"Old Hui muttered, "I don't care, *La Marseillaise* or whatever, key change or no key change, I'm only playing it in C."

As Shi Zhaochang watched the great man of patriotic music walk away, there was something he couldn't figure out: why were the faces of heroes always so white, and their hair so shiny? The way the women were all arguing and laughing with the men make him look down on them, but then again The Woman Warrior of National Salvation was one of them too. She was just talking about national salvation through song and dance, not about warrior issues.

He just had to go away with her to do good deeds! He had already studied with The Supreme Ultimate Master for four or five days, so he only needed another ten days or so before he could go and do great things. Just so as The Woman Warrior of National Salvation hadn't let her martial gongfu go rusty.

"Her external and internal gongfu both seem good, but it doesn't seem that she is very diligent. She doesn't..."

Miss He was busy for a long time before catching a breath and sitting down in a chair next to him. He gave her arm a pinch: So very soft, anyone could tell she knew internal gongfu.

"Let me ask you," Shi Zhaochang brought his lips close to Miss He Manli's ear. "These people, these...these... They... The men and the women are so... They are all so..."

Shanghai's Thirteenth Sister was just as clever as the one from Tianqiao: She immediately knew what he meant. While applying her makeup in the mirror, she straightened her back and set forth.

"That's modern culture!" She raised her voice so that anyone could hear her. "We want to promote our cause, we're for our new morality: Openly fraternizin', freedom of love, dancing, patriotism, golf playing, the democratic spirit, perms, the romantic school, we're fer all that stuff. So all the boys want to be modern, put Stacomb in their hair and go looking for a sugar momma, and all the girls want to be a modern *gerl*..."

"*gerl*?"

"*Gerl*. G-I-R-L. So we're all agin the old ethics. Look, the industry of the old Stars 'n Stripes is really developed, that's why the Stars 'n Stripes is so modern, so rich and strong. We Chinese have to do all we can to promote industry, to modern-up! That's the only way we can beat those Nip bastards. China has to..."

Shi Zhaochang gasped out, "Promote industry to beat the devils? Not through warriors?"

"That too: I'm doing *Woman Warrior of National Salvation* in just a sec! Oh yeah... now I'm doing *China, I Love You*! You'd better go and watch!"

But he recalled another thing he had to ask her: "Did you just say something about tearing down the old something-or-other?"

"Tear down the old what? Oh, yeah, I said we have to tear

down the old ethics: We gotta trust in industry to save the nation, tear down superstition. We need revolution in the family, we gotta promote dignity, that's it."

The man stared at her hard: He suspected he might be dreaming. How, after all this time, this Woman Warrior of National Salvation is following the Path of Evil!

Many men and women crowding around had heard Miss He's comments, and they all applauded. Miss He's gave her conclusion:

"So we all gotta promote modern song and dance to save the nation!"

Everyone shouted, "Long Live The Modern Patriotic Song and Dance Troupe!"

Shi Zhaochang was dripping sweat as the tips of his fingers started to go cold.

"Have I been seduced by the Path of Evil? Is she acting like she is evil on purpose to test me?"

In a flash, he stood and, not caring about his situation, cried out, "Evil! Evil! This is evil! I must subdue it! I must..."

When the others tried to drag him outside to watch *China, I Love You*, he dropped into a Horse Stance and refused to budge, so they just dumped him in the floor seating.

He nearly fainted. Hands lifted up his swollen head. Someone seemed to be poking and prodding at his five viscera. He had gone from Miss He, the Woman Warrior of National Salvation, coming to his home, to the thrown mud-pellet, to handing over thirty dollars, to facing off lip to lip in a contest of skill, to that last evil speech.

"Evil! Evil!" he spoke to himself feverishly. "The Woman Warrior looks down on me and did this on purpose. How did I fail her? What did I do wrong?"

But he couldn't figure out what he had done wrong no

matter how he thought about it. He hadn't failed her. He had done everything by the book: he loved her, that's why he gave her the money, just like it was written in that *Something Destiny* book. Did he give her enough?

Ah, how awkward!

Lots of heads in the floor seating looked up and cheered. People stood and blocked the view of the stage and were shouted down by people behind them: "Sit down! Sit down!" They sat down grumbling.

On stage, the girls gigglingly danced for a while, then, with strained voices, they belted to the audience, "China, I love you! I love you. I love you. I love your Maaaaaanchuria. Soooooo big. Soooooo wide. Tiny little JXpan—How could it coooompare-are-are. Hey! How could they coooompare..."

All Shi Zhaochang could do was lower his head, close his eyes and suffer his thoughts. He heard a sudden noise. He thought it must be a howling cat, but gradually he was able to make out some words from the wailing.

"Ah! It's a woman crying for help!" He kept his eyes closed and listened with all his heart.

That's it! The sound of a woman being wronged and crying out for her life!

Suddenly, in a flash, instantly—but none of those words can describe the speed. In any case, it was really really fast. He stood up. He took his stance, left hand over his eyes to guard against the light, eyes searching every corner up and down: He wanted to find where that call for help was coming from. He had to right the injustice.

"Hey, buddy, sit down," someone behind him tapped his lightly.

Shi Zhaochang saw where the call was coming from: Ha! On the stage!

"Oh, it's a song," He sat down gently.

Onstage the bleating continued, "I love your Yangtze River…"

That Great Man of Patriotic Music Mr. Hui was busy playing that foreign instrument, with snot running down and no time to wipe it. Only after he was finished did he pull out a colored handkerchief and wipe his nose and mouth, his face full of pride as he looked down from the stage.

"That's Evil! That!" Shi Zhaochang thought as pain rose in his heart. "No matter who it is. If it is fucking Evil, I Shi Zhaochang must…"

Right then a good-looking man in a jade-green necktie called out a greeting from afar, and then he came near. Ah, it's Liu Zhao.

"I saw you earlier," Liu Zhao greeted his with clasped hands. "This kind of song and dance is no good. Very inferior to what you would see abroad, isn't that so?"

He snorted with condescension.

Liu Zhao leaned with his right hand on the back of the chair, rubbing his back with his left hand, all the while talking about the foreigners' beautiful performances. Then he said that he planned on watching the rest of the performance and then he would invite Shi Zhaochang out for drinks. He had raised his voice quite loud, otherwise Shi Zhaochang wouldn't have been able to hear him—the place was so noisy with people clapping and cheering, urging the curtain to open for the second act.

Liu Zhao leaned close to Shi Zhaochang's ear and shouted, "I'm incredibly lonely. Brother Zhaochang, would you be willing to accompany me for a tipple?"

Shi Zhaochang could not cast away The Woman Warrior of National Salvation. But then again, he should deliberately cast her away. Was she actually Evil or not? He must not wrong a good person. But to be seduced by the Path of Evil wasn't anything to take lightly either. Fine, fuck it, leave and deal with it later. Tomorrow he could look into it in detail.

He lips trembled. "I'm bored to death too, I'm also... dammit, people trying to put one over on me... Fine, go drinking. Your place?"

"My place, ah, the Campaign Against the Barbarians Fund Committee."

But Shi Zhaochang still hesitated. Should he let her know— tell that woman whose fate was tied up with his?

"Fate!" When he thought of that word—fated enemy or fated lover—his face reddened. She loved him. But she seemed a little...

"I won't tell her!" He clenched his teeth. "If she is on the Path of Evil, she will understand me already..."

He stood up with force and followed Liu Zhao out.

It was strangely cold outside.

As he two of them left the theatre several lower class people blocked them:

"Sir, contribute some money?"

Shi Zhaochang felt that something wasn't right. Lower-class people by their nature were bad at heart. And moreover— They were demanding money! Today was so strange. Just now, The Woman Warrior of National Salvation was like that, and now...

He placed all his force into his arms and declared:

"What is all this then?"

"We're workers at the XX-run Hongfa Company. We want to destroy XX Imperialism, we want to give them a real... We want to go on strike..."

Strike! It was another ploy of the Path of Evil!

"Haha! Strike!" Shi Zhaochang laughed maliciously.

"We want to go on strike to the end: no matter where it ends up. Against the Imperialist bastards to the very end… But we have to ask everyone for help, right now we don't even have enough money for food…"

They grit their teeth: without help, they would all starve to death, or else they couldn't help but go back to work from hunger. It was not at the critical moment. They were flexing their arms, but their lips trembled.

"If we don't have ten copper each per day then we can't struggle on. Without that, people will go back to work. If… If…"

The person speaking looked around, trying to keep tears from falling. He bit his lip and his cheek twitched.

The cold wind blew in like it had eyes, and Shi Zhaochang lifted the collar of his long gown to protect his neck. Liu Zhao put his two delicate hands in his pockets. They looked at each other. Neither knew how to handle this.

"The elite families are also on a hunger strike to save the nation." Liu Zhao muttered under his breath.

Shi Zhaochang let all of the force from his arms where he had so recently put it. He had to figure this out. To go on a strike was the Path of Evil. But they were striking against the devils. Should he give them a few coins or not? He had to decide quickly: it was too cold to just stand around here.

"This is the method of using Evil to fight the Path of Evil," he argued to himself. "Perhaps it is the Jade Emperor using this Evil to destroy the devils."

Well then, he would do his part. He stuck out his belly and patted it with his right hand. "I'm Shi Zhaochang. I, Shi Zhaochang have always distributed funds for noble causes, no matter how much, but you must explain everything clearly, yes. I must know precisely your background. If you explain everything clearly, then I, Shi Zhaochang shall donate—one *mao*, two—I couldn't care less... Come now let us see. I ask you: The XX devils are of the Path of Evil, yes?"

"What's the Path of Evil?"

Ah! They didn't even know of the Path of Evil!

"I ask you: Why is it that the XX devils have come to fight our China?"

"There're a few wretches that wanted to come to China to make foreign money."

Shi Zhaochang looked at them. There was something not quite right in the way they spoke. If they were Evil, Shi Zhaochang would need to subdue them here. He patiently continued his questions:

"Are there good people among the XX devils?"

One of them grinned in a flash: "There's good ones and bad ones."

Another one broke in: "Last time they had the Town Hall Meeting, there were those two XX guys who gave a speech: They wanted to take down the XX Imperialist bastards too. They called us "brothers," "Don't fight our Chinese brothers.""

Liu Zhao didn't say anything but put on a bored expression and stood further away. He didn't understand why Shi Zhaochang wanted go on with them: If someone they knew saw this what would they say?—grumbling inanities with those people like they were friends! But it was like a strong hand was pulling him closer, and he couldn't help wanting to speak.

He hadn't thought it out properly yet though. It was good of course that Japan would soon be destroyed. They had riled themselves up into a real mess: Lots of people opposed the government, they were those unruly people. China had some rotten eggs too. That was dangerous. But...

"They are splitting apart from within their nation. They will fall on their own." He thought. That made him happy. But it would be too dangerous if those unruly people in China...

He suddenly remembered that he was standing in front of those people in their tattered coats. Perhaps they were unruly. He drew his hands out of his coat pockets with force. He made a gesture:

"That is the Ethnic Essence of the XX! Their Ethnic Essence is to be forever capricious. Some of them will want to "take down XX Imperialism," but you can't trust them. Those people are unruly people. As soon as people like that take over, this China of ours will be even more of a disaster. Our Chinese... Chinese..." His hands were cold. He put them back in his pockets. "Our China...China...If those unruly XX take over, we Chinese will also have to... There'll be nothing good for us Chinese, don't you see. Those devils all... They...so if those unruly XX devils take over China is done for, don't you see. That's why this... this... this..."

The speaker stuck out his chest and fixed everyone with his gaze. He had suddenly remembered the phrase that orators used when they finished and stepped down from the stage. With a firm determination: "Our position is precisely this! There is nothing more!"

Shi Zhaochang ended up talking about the strike with the men. This had to be the Will of Heaven using Evil to fight Evil. Who could say that the Jade Emperor might not have issued an edict, and the Will of Heaven must not be infringed. He reached into his pocket.

"I, Shi Zhaochang, have always fought against injustice. I, Shi Zhaochang, distribute funds for noble causes. Remember this: The surname is Shi, called Shi Zhaochang. I bestow two *mao* in cash—Two *mao*! Hm, I ask you: do you publish a record of the names of the people who have donated in the papers?"

"Published in the papers?"

"Yes," his right hand lingered in the pocket. "Who donates and how much, who donates and how much, the names should all be published, that plus gratitude."

"How would we have the money left to publish in the papers?"

"That's unacceptable. If you don't publish it, the benefactors will have donated in vain: names must be made known to everyone." Shi Zhaochang's right hand moved in his pocket, and ten or so dozen pairs of eyes watched with keen attention for it to emerge: It did not.

"The names must be published. Money is of no matter: Since time immemorial, I, Shi Zhaochang, have distributed funds for noble causes. Everyone knows this." The right hand moved a bit but again, did not emerge. "I ask you: What is your name?"

The one closest to him, holding the donation box looked at him. "I am Hou Changchun."

Shi Zhaochang rubbed his face. Of course, he used his left hand, as his right was still in his pocket.

"I ask you: Whatever did you go to work in the devil's factory for anyway? What did you do before?"

Hou Changchun and the rest were trying to keep their patience. No matter what he was pulling, he had promised twenty cents. If they bought sesame cakes, that twenty cents could feed three or four people for a day. All they needed to do was swallow this, and they could fight to the end and wouldn't have to go back to work. Hou Changchun forced down his temper and blew out a mouthful of air. He very carefully told what he used to do, but the tone of his voice was a little unnatural. His gaze was locked on the two gentlemen.

"Before, I was a farmer in the countryside. If you would like to know the size of our land rental, each year…"

A farmer! It was as if roiling steam suddenly boiled up in Shi Zhaochang's belly, blowing his entire body into pieces. He gasped, and his eyes bulged as his teeth ground together.

"Damnit, great! A Farmer!"

He had never dealt with laborers: they had nothing to do with Good or Evil. All he wanted to do was fight a little injustice. But farmers! At the beginning of this year, they farmers were all… they were all…

Shi Zhaochang recalled how his own family suffered at the hands of tenant farmers: the tenant farmers would go to the county to bring cases against the Shi Family, saying they were being abused. They would bring petitions too. They wouldn't allow the Shi family to raise rent. They would descend like a swarm of wasps demanding the granary be opened to appease justice, and sometimes they would go straight to stealing rice. There was one of them that actually hung herself in the Shi Family compound which ended up in a murder suit.

The Shi Family had suffered so much at the hands of farmers!

Now there wasn't a single good one among farmers, they are all depraved and degenerate! Farmers! How many of you used to be farmers?

That is what he said in front of the man called Hou Changchun!

Shi Zhaochang stared until his eyes started to ache. Veins started popping up all over his face. His lips paled. Suddenly he shouted out: He was normally somewhere between a bass and baritone, but this time his voice was a high tenor and when it came to his throat, it exited in a screech.

"Evil! Bandits! You've caused me such suffering! Fuck a million generations of your ancestors!"

In a flash, he stepped back a few paces, bent his legs and took a stance. His right hand came out of his pocket. There was nothing in it, but he was acting like he could use the Five Thunder Strike technique. He thrust out his head and hunched up his back. He stretched out his neck quite long, making the skin of his neck bizarrely taut.

Liu Zhao was frightened—no, that's not right, Liu Zhao didn't have time to be frightened. Shi Zhaochang took up another stance: He advanced on Hou Changchun and the rest with a Form-Intention stride. As one foot stepped closer, his hand rose forward. He was about one step away from Hou Changchun, and Shi Zhaochang's neck was stretching out even longer. His mouth tightly shut, he stared forcefully at Hou Changchun to the point that his eyeballs nearly popped out of their sockets. Staring like this, he ferociously leapt out.

His opponent had fled a very long time before this point.

That is to say that Shi Zhaochang leapt into thin air. Shi Zhaochang then leapt into a wall. His own ferocity then fell upon his own body, and he then fell to the ground.

A massive bump started to raise on the top of his head.

Everything in front of his eyes swayed back and forth. There were little colored bits of paper flying everywhere. They danced in the electric lights.

What? This is...

They used Evil sorcery! Ah!

He had to reach down and use his true power: The Supreme Ultimate Master taught him the incantations that could dispel evil magic, but The Supreme Ultimate Master told him that he couldn't use such power casually. "Only as a last resort, don't you know. For example, if you are fighting the devils, then you can use this magic."

"Dammit!" Shi Zhaochang pulled himself up, and using that high-pitched voice, "You used Evil sorcery! Evil sorcery! Your damned old man will show you something…"

He balled up his fists and started punching out toward Hou Changchun and the rest with all his might.

Liu Zhao tried to hold him back, but couldn't. Liu Zhao grabbed him from behind. "Brother Zhaochang, stop fighting, stop fighting, Brother Zhaochang!"

"Let me go. I have to beat those evil ones who go against goodness, I have to beat them to death!" With a great twist, Shi Zhaochang and Liu Zhao both tumbled to the ground.

Many people had gathered around to watch the commotion. Police who were on post came over too. They lifted Shi Zhaochang and Liu Zhao up to stand, and blocked Shi Zhaochang, not letting him show his skill again.

"What's going on, what's going on?"

"What're they doin? Whoa-ho, Beating up some playboy!"

"I have to go and beat those evil-doers to death! They used Evil sorcery, look!"

"We asked him for a donation. Nothing at all, for no reason, he started attacking us. We didn't even… absolutely nothing…"

Liu Zhao looked at the patrolmen and raised his voice, "You workhands—they started the fight!"

"What? We attacked him? It was him…"

"Shut your blabbering!" The policeman interrupted them. Turning to Liu Zhao, "You are…"

"They attacked us!"

"We…we… Ah… All of you, look, this man…"

"They're trouble from the day they're born! Troublemakers! Swine! Wretches! Bastards! Bad elements! Just one look at them and you can tell that they're criminals in the making! What could they possibly…"

As Liu Zhao was delivering this tirade of curses, he noticed that his coat was covered in ash, as he focused on patting it off.

The people who had come to watch the commotion looked at the clothes of Shi Zhaochang and Liu Zhao—their clothes were about the same as the crowd's, so they immediately knew their western-dressed friends couldn't be in the wrong. They looked at Hou Changchun, "Just one look at them and you can tell…"

"Asking for donations is one thing, but to attack someone?!"

"Those two! Arguing with those… It's not worth the trouble!"

"Iffn'ya fight 'n' win that's one thing, but ya lose and get the worst of it, ain't worth it, yeah?"

"Yeah!" A middle-aged man drawled out in a Wuxi accent. Everyone stared at him.

"Let's beat it!" giggled a kid, before sticking out his tongue and slipping away.

The policeman sighed and with unexpected friendliness, told Hou Changchun and his people they could leave.

"Ok, ok, ok. Go somewhere else to ask for donations."

Everyone knew that there wasn't going to be a show worth watching, so they left one by one.

After that, Liu Zhao and Shi Zhaochang headed to the street. Liu Zhao puffed out his chest and kept his mouth shut tight. Shi Zhaochang was in a bad temper: Thinking back on the discussion with The Woman Warrior of National Salvation, thinking back on the donation for building that platform for refining immortality pills at Mount Kunlun, thinking back just then at those Evil men. He remembered some Shanghainese curses and set about using them.

"It's just beyond the pale! Dunce! Whoreson! Evil! Conmen! Bastards!"

9

The Secret of Spending Money in Fighting For Justice

LIU ZHAO OFTEN CAME to see Shi Zhaochang. This time he had changed his tie: it was now purple with light green dots. He twice invited Shi Zhaochang to eat dough noodle soup with him, and took him to the Campaign Against the Barbarians Fund Committee. His plan was to get Shi Zhaochang to donate a thousand or two.

Shi Zhaochang's face reddened. "I don't have any money. Father's the only one with money."

"Uncle Shi has donated already," Liu Zhao brought his hands together with great curtesy. "You do have money. You have your bank passbook in your hand, for you to use as you please. I know that."

What a disaster! Who told him that?

How could he know if someone didn't tell him? He just told Shi Zhaochang about the importance of the Campaign Against the Barbarians and that the entire nation had to donate a bit to the cause. The people in the Campaign Against the Barbarians Fund Committee were extremely patriotic, and everyone worked hard. As he went on talking he took out a Garrick and gave it to Shi Zhaochang, and then from a folder he took out an organization chart of the Campaign Against the Barbarians Fund Committee to let Shi Zhaochang look over.

"This is our organization chart. We have a lot of patriotic activities."

With a heavy draw on the cigarette, Shi Zhaochang took the folder. On the cover was written again, "The Imprint of Le Lezhai, Doctor of Literature." It was quite thick, and on one hundred twenty pound paper, around five hundred pages for the whole book. Foreign bound. Rounded gilt spine.

He couldn't read it all at once, so Liu Zhao flipped through to the organization chart for him, and with an oddly graceful gesture, he pointed with his right hand to the top of the chart:

"Now, that's the standing committee: that's the highest. It's got... Underneath is split into five ministries. Under the ministries are the offices. Under the offices are, uh, this section and that section belong to the offices. Under the sections, they're divided into units. And there are two other committees—they aren't considered cadres. Ah, this line here comes down here, they're directly subordinate to the standing committee... All told there are only six hundred staff, we never have enough people... Expenses are heavy, but we can't ask the government for funding, and we can't ask the ordinary people for money. We are..."

He stopped. When he started again it was with less focus. He quickly smoked several cigarettes. Then he jumped up and concluded:

"So there is only one way out for our people: we must focus on the Campaign Against Barbarians Fund. We must campaign against the barbarians. Exterminate all the savages! Must conquer... conquer... conquer these..."

He hadn't finished his conquering when a servant-looking person came to stand in the doorway and announce:

"Mr. Liu, Office Director Le asks to see you."

"Office Director Le wants to see me? Ah... Brother

Zhaochang have a seat, I'll be right…"

Shi Zhaochang sat alone smoking and looking around. He thought about the finances: Whose pocketbook were this Campaign Against the Foreigners Fund Committee's huge expenses coming out of? Mr. Liu Liu and those people?

"Enthusiasm is all good, but it's of no use! Just look!"

He stood up. He recalled the Passing Through Earth incantation The Supreme Ultimate Master taught him, but he couldn't remember the third phrase.

"Have to put in a little effort," he said to himself.

He had studied all sorts of magic. All he had left was to study Spitting Blades. Ha! Just think! In just a few days, he and Thirteenth Sister…… The image of The Woman Warrior of National Salvation flashed in his mind and there was an ache in the pit of his heart.

He ambled out the door.

"Fuck it. Anyway it's all fate. If she is on the Path of Evil, then I won't be easy on her. If she is Good, then things can be done with her… with her…"

There was a sudden burst of laughter from the opposite office.

What? Did they know what was in Shi Zhaochang's heart?—He had to hear what they were talking about.

"Of course Old Ren is doing well here as a seventh rank section worker: This month he took in seven hundred dollars, and there's the bonus. Where could a secretary have it more comfortable than here?"

"But this month is a good month."

"Good month? This doesn't even count as a good month. We'll get another five hundred-some thousand in Campaign Against the Barbarians donations from the South Seas, and then…"

"Is it really that much?"

"Of course."

"I doubt it."

"How can you doubt it? I've seen the telegrams."

"Um, then with the bonus, every one of us will have—two and seven, fourteen, six and six, thirty-six, and then another thousand…"

"So you have to send Miss He to the Nichang store to have some clothes made."

"And there's more good news."

After this there was silence, as if the reporter of good news wanted to keep the listener in suspense.

Shi Zhaochang moved closer to the office door, not letting out even the sound of his breath, to hear the 'good news' from inside the office.

It was this:

"Committeeman Liu and them were worried that we didn't have a regular fee while they are asking the entire nation to donate to the Campaign Against the Barbarians fund every month. All the staff in the organization have their donation taken out of their pay, it's taken out according to their salary, ten or twenty percent. The students all over the nation put in a little too. It all gets collected right here."

"It's so clever, then… Ah, we need to raise salaries."

"We would have to get the government to agree to that, you think they'd be willing?"

"We represent the public will of the citizens of the nation, of course the government would have to agree… That way we would have a regular income. Otherwise, uh, when we run into a bad month, we won't be able to scrape up a penny. A soon as we get a regular income, then we won't have to worry about anything. Each and every month would be set, and Old

Chu can have clothes made for Miss He every month."

More peals of laughter.

"This is an excellent plan. The staff salaries here at the Campaign Against the Barbarian Fund Committee can go up. That's number one. Number two, if we, for example, have a really good month, like, if the overseas Chinese donate a few hundred thousand or a million, then more bonuses. Naturally, we on the committees are enthusiastic: Utterly upright and candid, the finances are completely open."

"Long live the Campaign Against the Barbarian Fund Committee!"

"If the Campaign Against the Barbarian Fund Committee can survive forever, I'll never have to work a day more in my life!"

Silence for a while.

"Right, Old Chu, how did that thing I asked you about last time go?"

"What thing?"

"Ah ha! Have you forgotten?"

"Oh, you want to get in the Hunger Strike of the Famous National Salvation Group, that's it, right?"

"Yeah."

"No way, no way, no way! Mr. Liu Liu got upset: 'He wants in, he wants in.' How can we have so many "elite" people around? There need to be qualifications here. How can people just stumble in—putting their names right next to the names of the elite, they don't rank! He also said, "I'm giving up food like this for the good of the nation. I wish I weren't elite. What's so great about dough noodle soup? All of you non-elite people just love to go on hunger strikes! There are many ways to save the nation, and the best is to do your all in donating to the Campaign Against the Barbarians." After all that, how could I mention it?"

After a while, they went back to talking about the Campaign Against the Barbarian Fund.

Shi Zhaochang was at a loss. His thoughts about the Campaign Against the Barbarian Fund Committee were spinning around in his head, and he just couldn't think it through.

"So is this Evil or Good?"

That evening Mr. Liu Liu sent a message to invite Shi Zhaochang to have dough noodle soup and some drinks, but Shi Zhaochang resolutely declined to go out. Liu Zhao followed him and tried to make a donation.

"Bother Zhaochang, you still haven't donated to the Campaign Against the Barbarian Fund. Surely you don't think our people are already destroyed?"

"How did you know about my money? Who told you?"

"I just knew it. It's the ethnic essence of my people. Shi Zhaochang, just donate a couple of thousand."

Then the words came awkwardly:

"I have to... I have to... This... I don't have any... I, Shi Zhaochang, spend money in the fight for justice, I am... But I must... I am considering..."

Shi Zhaochang wanted to complain about his father: It had to be him that told Liu Zhao. His father and Liu Zhao were ganging up on him.

Actually, Mister Shi Boxiong didn't have that idea at all. He had only mentioned Shi Zhaochang's savings in detail to Mrs. Shi. Mrs. Shi rather unfairly told this to Mrs. Liu. Mrs. Liu comforted Mrs Shi, but joked about it to her son Liu Zhao:

"Why don't you ask Young Master Shi to donate some?"

That's how Liu Zhao knew.

Now warriors don't care about lucre, but you still want

to get your money's worth. "Money doesn't come easy," Shi Zhaochang remembered his father often said. Shi Zhaochang's grandfather toiled his entire life as an official before he was able to buy that land. Till his dying day, you couldn't say he carelessly spent a single penny. His father was his father's true son, always bringing this up: using this method, in one year, he could take in eight hundred piculs of grain, and the next year he would have sixteen hundred piculs. One dollar this month becomes two the next month.

There was a method in this. The Elder Shi Boxiang added a lot of land to his holdings. And he left some in cash: A banker encouraged him to do this, "Land can't be relied on now." How true! Now they couldn't go back home. Everything they wore and ate, depended entirely on the interest from that cash.

"You must remember," the Elder Mr. Shi said to Shi Zhaochang, "the only reason we have what we have today is all because of one word: 'thrift.'"

The Elder Mr. Shi then talked about the method to spending:

"You have to understand: the only thing that is most important in this world is property. In spending money, you have to think about whether there is benefit or not: if you spend a dollar, you are a dollar in debt—can you make that back? How much is the return on your money, all these things you must carefully consider, consider over and over again. For example, inviting people to dinner... inviting... inviting can't be done casually: To invite once gains one invitation's worth of use... That is all to say, at every last moment, you must be thinking about the return on your money..."

At this the old man smiled and wiped those few strands of beard with a folded handkerchief. He had the secret and wonderful method of making money from his ancestors. He himself felt he could serve as the minister of finance. He had to pass down this method to his children. He talked again about the marvels of compound interest. Ah, not a hint of carelessness in this expert, this father.

"One dollar becoming two, that added dollar is interest. Wealthy men throughout the world have all relied on return on investment to become wealthy: For example, that Zhang from Tongzhou who came in first in the exams, or that English oil king, that steel king…"

"The oil king and the steel king are French, not English."

"Not English?" The old man wasn't happy at being interrupted

"Eh, doesn't matter, the point is they all relied on this: Compound Interest. I'll give you another example: Worshiping the Buddha and praying to the gods. Hmph. There's huge return there. You spend a dollar to buy a silver ingot, spend another dollar to buy a joss stick. That's two dollars all told now. You pray for the bodhisattva to watch over you and make you rich—for example, to make a hundred dollars. That's a ninety-eight dollar return. If you go to the altar and pray for Lu Yan to be your master, I am… That is… oh, oh, oh.. eh?"

Needless to say, it was all return on investment.

"For food and clothes now, you never want to use the capital, you understand?... Zhaochang, tell me: If you don't use capital, what do you use?"

"Interest."

"Ai! That's right! That's right!" Father slapped the desk then pulled Shi Zhaochang over to pat him on the back. "That's right! That's right! Use the interest. Ai, that's right! Capital can be used up. But even when using the interest, you can't use it blindly: Interest can also bring more interest, don't you know."

When Shi Zhaochang was a little older, The Elder Mr. Shi told him that "return on investment" could be explained in many ways.

"For example, if you donate a hundred dollars to disaster relief, is it not the case that that hundred dollars has no return? And even the principal cannot be regained. But in this there is principal and interest! But it is not in money, but in reputation. And there are times when it builds face to spend money. Understood? Reputation and face are very important: with reputation and face, days go by much more smoothly. This is an extraordinarily large return on investment. For example, I... For example, I... I am now..."

What he stuttered out was this: spending money leads to reputation and face. To have reputation and face makes it easier to move about in society. The wealthiest people are the most active in society.

What Shi Zhaochang understood of this secret method of his ancestors was this:

"Spending money must have a benefit, that's it, right papa?"

"Right! You can understand it just like that. It's no wonder the fortune teller says that you will be a great hero! Even great heroes have to spend money."

"Even great heroes have to spend money." That was how Shi Zhaochang spent money. But if the Campaign Against the Foreigners Fund Committee was such a useless thing, any money set out wouldn't bring anything back. There were many things to spend money on: The Supreme Ultimate Master—there was a big outlay.

"Of all the things about being a warrior, this is the only awkward one," he thought.

Why did that rule have to be set down! Spending money in

fighting for justice!

But that outlay for his Master, that was necessary.

But he only gave a hundred dollars, he had to wait for the rest. It seemed that he was waiting for his master to teach him a bit of the Dao, and then he would pay off the rest. The Supreme Ultimate Master was very upset:

"Disciple! Third Disciple Bowen came to Shanghai yesterday with a payment. The altar on Kunlun Mountain is…"

"I'll get it tomorrow or the day after. These past few days, the banks… The banks have been so… I went, I went… go…"

Every morning he went to The Supreme Ultimate Master's to train for two hours. He couldn't avoid paying. But that money—One more day in the bank was one more day worth of interest!

The Supreme Ultimate Master at the Altar Hall of the Three Teachings, not far from the bank where Shi Zhaochang had his money. Every time he walked past the door of the bank, his heart would start pounding for some unknown reason.

"I should just pick a day to give him that three thousand nine hundred dollars," he debated with himself. Three thousand nine hundred dollars!

On the ninth day of training, Shi Zhaochang wrote a check and gave it to his master. He wanted to ask his master for a receipt, but didn't know how to bring it up.

The Supreme Ultimate Master stuffed the check in his pocket with complete disregard and took Shi Zhaochang to another room to impart Daoist Arts. Only the master and disciple were in the room. The door was securely bolted so that a third party couldn't see or hear. It was like this every day.

And what did that disciple learn?

We have no way of knowing. "Official Top Secret."

There were two other people who saw The Supreme Ultimate Master put the check in his pocket: Elder Brother Hu Genbao and Elder Brother Disciple Half Mote. Their four eyes locked on their master until he was out of sight.

Hu Genbao said something in Half Mote's ear and the two of them sat down outside that closed door.

The Hall of the Three Teachings used to be a temple, established by a great man from Hunan who died seventy years ago. The rooms of the temple had never been maintained, so the wind would blow through the wall partitions. Half Mote was shivering with cold.

"These rooms are horrible," he mumbled. "We Hunanese have rich people here in Shanghai too. How is it that no one put up some cash to fix this place up?"

"Huh. You can do it." Hu Genbao's eyes darted forward toward the building with the altar.

"Me?" Half Mote chuckled. Then he pointed at the door with his thumb.

Hu Genbao's eyes hadn't moved an inch. He was watching the women kowtow: when they knelt, their butts looked bigger. Some of them were quite experienced at it. Some didn't get the posture quite right: as if they were still a little shy. Hu Genbao thought, "That woman must have a certain illness that needs a prescription."

The ladies all bowed to the table. On the table was a large tray with dirt in it. Kuai Sixteen and that one with the singed beard held a T-shaped thing and were focused on writing in the dirt. Hu Genbao, looking at this with all air of propriety, just laughed.

Elder Brother Disciple Half Mote looked at the floor and said to himself:

"If I donated some, I could ask Old Master Shi—Elder

Mister Shi Boxiang to donate some too. That would be a deed of highest merit. Old Master Shi would certainly donate. Old Master Shi is like us…"

"Hm, hm," Hu Genbao quickly interrupted with snorts. "Old Mister Shi is a benevolent man."

"Old Master Shi would be willing to put out money, he's not stingy. Old Master Shi is really… really…"

He made a gesture and so didn't need to keep talking. Half Mote changed tone:

"Yeah, benevolent man. Old Master Shi is a benevolent man…"

They were talking about Old Mister Shi Boxiang! They were quite familiar with Shi Boxiang. How? Had they had dealings with that old man?

Yes, indeed. I had utterly forgotten to explain it.

The Supreme Ultimate Master had taken Elder Brother Disciple and Hu Genbao to the home of Shi Boxiang to be introduced to Old Mister Shi. Now, Old Mister Shi often went to the Alter Hall of the Three Teachings. He was a disciple of Ancestor Lu Chunyang. Sometimes he would take his wife and Zhaowu. He was oddly respectful toward The Supreme Ultimate Master. The Supreme Ultimate Master was a junior classmate of Ancestor Lu, so he would rank a generation higher than Elder Mister Shi Boxiang.

"Old Master Shi is really a good man," Half Mote looked Hu Genbao in the eyes. "If the Hall of the Three Teachings could get one hundred thousand dollars donated, that would be enough. Old Master Shi… Old Master Shi is… We could ask Old Master Shi to donate ten thousand… ten thousand…"

Hu Genbao's foot was so cold it started to shiver. He stood up and started pacing.

Ash-black clouds were piling up in the sky, like a huge

cooking pot was covering over the heads of humanity.

"It'll snow," Hu Genbao said.

The closed door began to open. The Supreme Ultimate Mater came out. Behind him followed Shi Zhaochang, head bowed, cautiously walking with the stride of the True Doctrine.

Elder Brother Disciple stood and saluted The Supreme Ultimate Master. Hu Genbao quickly stepped back and stood respectfully to the side, giving way to his master.

Shi Zhaochang made four kowtows to his master, then returned home. He thought his body felt warm after learning those things today.

"Ah, this four thousand dollars wasn't wasted…Spending Money in Fighting for Justice. There is good sense in it. It's no wonder that the immortals of the blade, and warriors and all the rest spend money in fighting for justice."

Suddenly, he felt that Elder Brother and Elder Brother Disciple were strangely adorable. Elder Brother with his long pointed face. Elder Brother Disciple with his bald head and hooked nose. Weren't they absolutely adorable? They had treated him really well. Master said that they would have to assist him.

His heart was about to pounding wildly, as if he were thinking about Thirteenth Sister…

But that day, Elder Brother and Elder Brother Disciple couldn't wait to see him go. They watched his figure until it exited the main gate, and then rushed to the room where master was sleeping.

Elder Brother Disciple shouted out, "Let's go get the money! Let's go get the money!"

"Hold on there, bud!" Hu Genbao stuck out his hand as if to block his way.

Master smiled. "Fuck your mother. This bald bulb has truly never seen money, one glimpse and..."

"Four thousand all together," Hu Genbao knocked on the table with his right forefinger. "How do we split it? Now is the time to have a talk."

"Kuai Sixteen over there..." Master uses a long blackened fingernail to dig at the rheum in his eye. "Kuai Sixteen and Singed Beard will need a bit of a cut."

"So just give them a hundred to split."

Elder Brother Disciple shouted out again. "Yeah, yeah. Give those two a hundred. The three of us can split the three thousand nine hundred evenly. Three one thirty-one."

"An even split?" Hu Genbao smiled coldly. "An even split? It was your better who found that Shi. This business was brought out by your better, and you want an even split?"

Master also put in his opinion: "The lightbulb gets one share less. The rest gets evenly split between Hu and me."

But Hu Genbao didn't agree. He said that he should get two thousand and the Master and Elder Brother Disciple could split the rest however they like, he didn't care.

Elder Brother Disciple stared, but his eyelids were as heavy as matted curtains and his eyes couldn't open too widely.

"How could I rate so little...little... little little..."

The Supreme Ultimate Master cackled in his throat. "I'm the one who did the most work, how could I get the small share..."

"This bit of business was brought out by your better. It was your better who thought all this through..."

"I won't take the small share. I'd rather break it all up. I'll go to that Shi guy and expose the whole thing, have all of you..."

"Expose? You would expose it?... You need to take care you

don't put your own life in danger!"

"Fuck your goddamn mother! My own life!... I won't take the small share! Shi is my disciple, he trusts me. I'll... I'll..."

Bam! Hu Genbao cracked Master in the mouth.

The two leaped at each other.

Elder Brother Disciple panicked: "Stoppit! Stoppit!!"

After about ten minutes, the master and disciple were left gasping at the end of the fight. A method of dividing the money was talked out. Elder Brother Disciple: five hundred. The two from the Hall of the Three Teachings: one hundred. The rest would be split between The Supreme Ultimate Master and Hu Genbao. Elder Brother Disciple bawled about it being too unjust, but Hu Genbao popped him in the mouth and the agreement passed with his unspoken approval.

But there was a bruise below Supreme Ultimate Master's forehead. Hu Genbao was bleeding quite a bit from the nose.

10

Warriors and the New Morality

THE WOMAN WARRIOR of National Salvation He Manli was waiting for Shi Zhaochang to send her some money again. He said with his own mouth that he would donate some more. But she hadn't even seen his shadow in several days.

"Why ain't he come?"

Based on her previous experience, she knew that Shi Zhaochang would return to her with a strange eagerness. And he would enthusiastically bring money too. And the amount of money wouldn't be small. Wasn't she a woman? According to the rules, Shi Zhaochang should do just that. This was exactly what she was talking about that day about that New Modern Morality.

But a warrior doesn't bother with this morality.

"He jist don't get the rules."

Miss He sighed and called a rickshaw.

"Why ain't you come by my place la?"

Shi Zhaochang stared blankly for a long while. His stomach started going all crazy. He didn't know what he should do. He was right in the middle of getting ready to go to The Supreme Ultimate Master's to train when this interruption came. But the awkwardness in his heart wasn't because of that. He still hadn't figured out clearly if this Woman Warrior of National Salvation was in fact, Evil or not. He also had actually missed her, and to have her just show up in front of his face out of nowhere, he didn't know if he should break into fury or happiness.

His heart was pounding like it couldn't go on.

Those eyes looking at him: How could he stare like that, not even bringing up the money?

She now knew she had to act—In the end everything was done in accordance with the rules of the New Modern Morality: She pounced.

Shi Zhaochang tried to get into a stance, but he didn't have enough time, and was wrapped up by the Woman Warrior of National Salvation. His chest gasped unevenly and his mouth gaped open for air. Her closed eyes, face tilted upward: the stench in Shi Zhaochang's mouth passed straight toward her nose. She wrinkled her brow and was getting ready to break away, but then thought again:

"For the new morality, I must hold on la!"

While holding on, she cracked open an eye to peek at Shi Zhaochang. He hadn't moved at all. She would have to make the first move again. She pressed he lips upward.

His heart pounded enough to shake her, as if someone had shaken the bedrock nearby. She remembered something: According to the rules, people who are kissing always gasp a bit. So she breathed short and quickly, like a dog in the heat of summer.

"I love ya la," She said using that throaty voice the song and dance troupe used when singing "China I Love You." "Why ain'tcha... Why... Why haven't you come to look for me?"

"No time," Shi Zhaochang said with a low voice, stealing a glance at the poster of Yue Fei on the wall.

The two sat on the sofa.

Shi Zhaochang exhaled a long breath. She probably wasn't Evil. Otherwise...

"That day you said la, you would donate... donate..."

"What?" He had forgotten about that.

Oh ho! He was acting like he doesn't know la! Without delay, she put her head underneath his chin. Her permed hair poked into his nostrils, and he sneezed, spattering her hair with mucus and spittle.

"Look at you la!"

Shi Zhaochang immediately felt she was even more adorable than before. He wrapped his right arm around her waist and planned to say so much, but he sat dumb for a while. He didn't know what he should say according to the rules.

"You... You you... I... together... together... gather our power... fight injustice... get rich and become heroes... study Passing Through Earth..."

Just then, a throaty cackle burst out from outside the window.

"Hahaha! Elder Brother has a girl in his room! They're... hahaha! Everyone, come look!"

Shi Zhaochang jumped up and ran to the window.

"You! What are you doing?"

"Shameless! You two..." Shi Zhaowu, outside the window was making an obscene gesture with two hands, then ran off laughing.

"Beast!" He thought about chasing after the boy and letting him know what's right and wrong, but his step-mother would be heard to deal with.

"Evil! Demonic! No class at all, and they say he'll be a division commander next year!"

"That, uh, was your brother?"

"hmph."

The Woman Warrior for National Salvation pulled his two arms and brought her lips up to his ear.

"Don't go angry la! Let's go and enjoy ourselves a bit...

come play with me la."

Shi Zhaochang smiled at Miss He, and bit his lip. His finger was shaking and he didn't know why.

On the wall, the clock sounded: Three thirty.

There was the sound of footsteps from the guest room. Shi Zhaochang pulls back his hands.

"Ah, three thirty. I won't be able to go over to Master's"

"Huh? What master?"

Shi Zhaochang wiped his face with his hand, glanced at the poster of Yue Fei, and with great solemnity, said, "The Supreme Ultimate Master."

She smiled at him and did a hula dance to get her body over to the sofa and pick up her bag. She carefully used a small mirror to powder her face.

"Thirteenth Sister uses makeup?" He asked himself.

Women Warriors must know the rules of Women Warriors.

A smile flashed across his face as he put his hands behind his back and paced the room, paying particular attention that his gait would satisfy the Woman Warrior of National Salvation. He strove to hunch his back, and splayed his feet out nearly horizontally.

"That brother of mine," he tried to appear utterly unconcerned, to let others know that this position was totally natural. "Anytime my brother comes up, I must get angry. He is the child of my step-mother.... Hm. They also say that he will make a great show next year. Just watch!"

"Don't he gotta... What school does he attend la?"

"Him?" the line of his mouth twisted. "Study?"

The door of the room opened a crack. A pair of red eyes looked in from the opening. No one in the room noticed.

Miss He's right hand was on the powder box. Her left hand held the little mirror: far away, then close. She made all sorts of poses with her face: raised, lowered, to one side. The scent of sandalwood powder flowed through the entire room.

The crack in the doorway slowly widened. Appearing: red eyes: two; big mouth: one. The mouth was smiling. The flesh of the gums was about to squeeze out and hang on the outside.

Nobody saw. Miss He was doing her work facing the mirror, and Shi Zhaochang was sneaking peaks at Miss He.

Suddenly, something flew at Miss He. Then the door crashed shut. Then the sounds of Shi Zhaowu's feet could be heard running off.

"Ah!" Miss He cried out, her hands going to her face.

The thing that had flown at her was a sardine can, with some of the juices still inside, which splashed all over Miss He's face. Places where the sandalwood powder was washed away showed dense freckles, like clouds parting to reveal the stars.

Shi Zhaochang was furious.

"Bastard!" He rushed out.

"Eh eh eh! Stap! Stap! Ah don wantcha…"

He had already bolted out of the room with gritted teeth.

"You no-good shit! Bastard!"

But he didn't see a trace of Shi Zhaowu.

"Donchoo be angry la! It ain't important la."

Shi Zhaochang was still unhappy. Not until Miss He started washing her face was he slightly better. But then he added, "I can't stay here. Let's go out for a walk. This house is simply…"

The other one was scrubbing with foreign soap and a will. Now we can see her original appearance: a color, like Shi Zhaowu, similar to a rotten buddha hand fruit. In some areas, greenish. Wrinkles popped up like a dried out orange peel. Lips blackened. Spots, large and small covered her face. There were no eyebrows.

Every day when she washed her face, she was a little uncomfortable. Old la! Like a sick person la! Like a deed person... Like a dead person la. Have to put on rouge add some eyebrows and keep up appearances la. She felt that she was nearly dead, but every week she had to go to the stores and buy all these things to build herself into something like a young vivacious girl.

What does it matter: Fooling herself?

She immediately explained things to herself in good Mandarin:

"This is the way it oughtta be: This is our modern culture la, this is the new morality, la."

Now she again recited these words like a mantra, and rushed to put the makeup back on.

Shi Zhaochang was muttering curses about Shi Zhaowu: "Simply not a human being! Animal! Mongrel! Bastard! Dunce! Whoreson! Cur!"

It went on like this for an hour and a half before they were ready to go out. Shi Zhaochang made it clear that he would have to get back quickly for dinner.

"I can't stay out too late. My father has invited Master to dinner."

"We can go dancing tonight, dancing's supah swell fun la!"

"I don't know how."

"I'll teachya la!"

"Ah, no good. My father invited Master to dinner. I should accompany him."

Miss He brought up the money again:

"Bring a little money out witchya. You said you were going to donate some money la."

"Ah, uh, But... but..."

This mood wasn't quite right...

"New morality!" She thought. No matter what, she didn't forget her new morality. She cuddled her head closer. This time, whether by chance or whatever reason, Shi Zhaochang smelled the scent of her cheek: Powder, along with the remaining smell of the sardine oil.

How could he not donate, this time, eh?

"Another twenty..."

"Twenty!" Miss He puffed out her cheeks, glancing at the mirror to make sure her pose was correct.

"Last time, I... I was... Now, I..." Shi Zhaochang said as he walked to the door.

The previously puffed cheeks flattened, and she followed him out. He was locking the door with a key. She licked her right forefinger and started counting the bills, one of which she took out with both hands to look at in better light to see if it was good.

Shi Zhaochang looked at her putting the money in her bag. Another twenty! Fifty altogether.

"Not too expensive," he said to himself.

In the future when they go out to do great deeds and fighting injustice, her mud-pellets would be a great help. All told he had only spent fifty in foreign dollars.

The Woman Warrior of National Salvation had a thought. She always had to ask this Shi to donate a bit more. Sitting in the rickshaw, her two hands grasped her purse tightly. She turned her head around to look at the rickshaw behind her, but couldn't see Shi Zhaochang. She huffed. After a while, she turned back again as if she were afraid Shi Zhaochang might have escaped.

That man simply didn't understand the rules at all la. No one in the world is that cheap! Really!

The rickshaws pulled up to a stop in the *longtang* alley,

and the man and woman were face to face. She didn't move. According to the rules, the man should come over and open the door. He didn't move. He had already given her fifty dollars, and wasn't going to always be made to pay.

The Woman Warrior of National Salvation smiled. "I don't have any change la."

"Hm?"

"You, ah... have any change la?"

"Just now... just now... you are... didn't I just give you twenty dollars?"

"That's in bills la. I don't have any change la."

"Go change them."

She didn't pay any attention to that jab, and simply popped open the door."

Shi Zhaochang's face flushed red like raw beef. He muttered something to himself while with a seeming great effort his right hand dug out two Guangdong double dimes.

"Sir, can you swap these out please? These coins are lead."

"Bullshit!" He glared at the two rickshaw drivers. "I, Shi Zhaochang... Everyone knows I spend money to fight for justice. Would I cheat you over twenty cents?"

"It really is lead. I'll hit it and you'll hear..."

"Get the hell out of here!" Shi Zhaochang bellowed. "How come I can't use a perfectly fine dime! Bastard!"

He walked toward the door, but the rickshaw drivers wouldn't let him go.

"What!" Shi Zhaochang dropped into his stance, measuring up his two opponents.

The two men didn't look like they would be hard to overcome. That young arm a rough one, breathing unevenly with his chest sticking out. At most he was Shaolin School. The older one looked dazed. Red nose, hunched back.

But who could say the old man might not have some internal gongfu…

Shi Zhaochang's eyes focused on the tip of the old one's red nose.

Internal gongfu—the old man might be a match! He didn't have time to pull a rickshaw and practice internal gongfu, did he?…

There was a sudden burst of women's voices from inside the doorway:

"Manli's back!"

"Old Tao's waitin' fer ya upstairs."

"Old Tao! Old Tao! Manli's come back!"

"Mary! Mary!"

"Old Tao's been waitin' forever!"

The warrior outside the door knit his brow. He thought of turning to look, but didn't dare. I feared the two rickshaw drivers would bolt if he relaxed one iota.

"Sir, please swap out the coin."

"Fuck your mother!"

A crowd gathered to watch the commotion.

If there was a fight, it wouldn't go well. Shi Zhaochang had been in his stance for a long time, and his legs were going soft. But right then he couldn't relax: You could never tell with Evil people, they might attack without warning.

"What's goin' on?" Someone asked.

The young rickshaw driver and Shi Zhaochang started talking all at once. Shi Zhaochang had more to say, so when the other went quiet, he still hadn't ended. He was going over and over about what kind of people they were and about their position.

"How could I, Shi Zhaochang, con these men out of twenty cents, I, Shi Zhaochang…"

"This lead coin is his, this guy wanted to roll us…"

Crack! A slap to the face of the young rickshaw driver.

"Fuck your ma!" He rushed at him for all he was worth, but others held him back, and he roared out.

A thirty-or-so year old woman looked at Shi Zhaochang, popped open her purse and handed a twenty cent coin to the rickshaw driver.

"There now. Go."

The red-nosed old man saluted her several times, looked back at Shi Zhaochang, muttered something and pulled his empty rickshaw away.

The young one threw the lead coin on the ground and spat out, "that's for you!"

The coin rolled into the groove at the side of the cement road—where the greasy sewage drained.

Shi Zhaochang didn't come out of his stance until the crowd had dispersed.

"Hehe, if you're giving it to me, I'll take it. Only a real idiot wouldn't."

Shi Zhaochang picked up the coin, wiped the grease off with his finger, and put it in his pocket. Then in one stride he moved through the door. He shut the door with a Taiji Quan "cloud hand".

"Mister Shi, welcome!" shrieked a bare-legged woman with a swing of her backside.

Mr. Shi didn't pay much attention to her. He rushed straight upstairs.

As soon as he pushed open the door, he felt like he had jumped in a barrel of ice water—his entire body froze solid.

11

Heartbreak

THE WOMAN WARRIOR of National Salvation's room was as it had been. Sofa. Table. Pink curtains. Copper bed—with the comforter drawn open at an angle. The wall was still covered with all those women in negligee. The coal in the stove was popping.

Everything was as it had been. On the sofa lounged the Woman Warrior of National Salvation. Her purse and embroidered handkerchiefs were on the table next to a milk glass.

Everything was as it had been, except... to the lap of the Woman Warrior of National Salvation was added a great hunk of a man.

Shi Zhaochang clenched his fists. His fingers went cold. His eyes popped out like a goldfish's, staring like he would never close them ever again. He panted for breath.

The hunk jumped up. He was half a head taller than Shi Zhaochang. His brows looked like they had been vigorously painted with a thick brush in a horizontal like right over his eyes. His eyes squinted down into two lines. He thick lips pushed out like a chicken gizzard. He glared at Shi Zhaochang, then looked at the Woman Warrior of National Salvation—as if to ask, "who is this?"

The woman batted her eyes at the hunk and shrugged her shoulders. Then, giggling at Shi Zhaochang, she said, "Please sit down la. Lemme introduce you la: This is Mi-suh-tuo

Tao…"

Silence.

Shi Zhaochang's body didn't move. His mouth didn't move. He didn't know what to say. He had never encountered this before. He took in a lungful of air and held it, but he accidentally let it out again with a loud gasp—

"Phooo!"

The two were surprised.

The women downstairs were noisily chattering away: Some were humming songs, others were complaining.

"How'd you go an let that poor sod up?"

"He jist went up himself, dint he?"

"Where's your eyes at? Your eyes?"

Another one was actually speaking good Mandarin:

"What a mess la! Mary's gunna give us what for!"

A moment passes.

"That stiff seems to be really taking it serious."

Shi Zhaochang understood some of what was said. What. Don't let that 'stiff' upstairs?

That Missed-Whatever-Tao, glared at Shi Zhaochang. With an effort, he thought about closing up those gizzard lips of his. But they wouldn't close: they always hung out of his mouth like that. His brow furrowed, two eyebrows became one.

"Please sit."

Shi Zhaochang did not sit.

The Woman Warrior of National Salvation loudly and politely said:

"Why ain'tcha sittin?"

"I must be going." Shi Zhaochang said with labored breath.

The hunk and the Woman Warrior of National Salvation looked at each other. The hunk let out a breath and sat his butt down on the sofa. With a smooth gesture he picked up the embroidered handkerchief and wiped the sweat from his brow.

Miss He nodded at Shi Zhaochang:

"Then I'll seeya later la"

"Wait," Shi Zhaochang's voice trembled. "There is something else we have to discuss. We... we..."

The four eyes locked on Shi Zhaochang. Shi Zhaochang rubbed his scalp, licked his lips and said nothing for a long time.

The others were waiting for him.

That Missed-Whatever-Tao abruptly stood up. Shi Zhaochang was startled and took a step back. Eh, maybe this guy...

Dear Reader can imagine: Of course, this warrior secretly got into his stance.

Be careful, hey! If you start a fight—You'll be disappointed!

But for a long while no one moved.

"What?..."

The hunk had only walked to the stove, opened the door and looked inside. Then he wiped his lips with his hand, and looked at the women in negligee on the wall. Then, oh! Look carefully! The guy put his hand in his pocket!

A secret weapon!

A secret weapon?

Uh, the guy pulled out a cigar.

"Damnit!" Shi Zhaochang blew a mouthful of air out of puffed cheeks.

Suddenly—

"If ya got sumptin to say... Something... why dontcha say it la?"

Ah, Shi Zhaochang had nearly forgotten the Woman Warrior of National Salvation was right there.

"Weh, weh, uh… Yeah, ah, We… we…"

"Spit it out la."

"I… I… We… I mean, we… We need to settle accounts."

"Settle accounts?!" The Warrior Woman of National Salvation considered if she should add a 'la.'

"Yes. Settle accounts, settle… settle… You owe me fifty dollars."

Miss He pushed her face up to him—there was a bit of a fishy smell.

"How do I owe you fifty dollars la. You donated that to the Modern Patriotic Song and Dance Troupe la. There's no account to settle la."

"We… we…" Shi Zhaochang peeked over at that Missed-Whatever-Tao. "Let's go outside and talk."

That hunk watched the two of them.

The stove popped and crackled.

All of a sudden there was a shout like an anguished cry for help from downstairs:

"I love your Yangtze River, ah, ah!..."

The Woman Warrior of National Salvation's matchstick legs stomped the beat, and, in a sing-song voice she said:

"Nuh-uh!. dong, dong dong. dong, dong dong, DONG, dong dong. DONG, dong dong!"

Shi Zhaochang's breathing was uneven. He rubbed his hands in bewilderment. He sat down on a chair without realizing it, still looking at the Warrior Woman of National Salvation. Ah, what trouble: Those gongfu novels never dealt with this. How should this be handled? He did have to make it clear. He took in a lung-full of air and did his best to calm himself, but when he started to speak he still stuttered:

"We…I despise Evil: You are… You are… We're over!... You've got another…got…"

He gazed at the hunk with hatred.

"What's so important 'bout that la?"

"At first... at first... We'd do good deeds together, but you... I can't love... I! I!"

My dear reader of course knows the position Shi Zhaochang is in. It is called: Heartbreak. It is said that heartbreak is painful, and so we should not wonder at this warrior's miserable visage. Shi Zhaochang was hurt, and not lightly. He wanted to drive off that hunk. He wanted to plead with the Woman Warrior of National Salvation never again to pay that hunk any attention, and not let him sit on her lap.

He stood up.

"Ah!" Miss He shrieked. As if she were afraid someone might hit her, she dashed to the hunk's side, and was going to nestle her head on his shoulder, but he was too tall, so she put her head on his chest, all the while peeking at her own pose—checking if it was pretty enough.

That Missed-Whatever-Tao knew what he was supposed to do: he put his arm around Miss He's shoulder, puffed out his chest and looked at Shi Zhaochang, stared at him.

Shi Zhaochang leaned on the table with his right arm.

"You...You..."

The Woman Warrior of National Salvation knew what Shi Zhaochang meant. She shrugged, straightened up and the corners of her mouth dipped. About ten seconds went by that way, and then she quickly spat out a mouthful of Mandarin:

"Don't be so stupid la! You donated fifty dollars la, and this Mi-suh-tuo Tao donated five hundred dollars la! You fifty dollars la! Fifty dollars gets fifty dollars' worth la! Don't think you're gunna eat swan la! I love 'im la! You jist don't understand even one little bit of morality la! You poor stiff la, you got no face la!"

Shi Zhaochang was struck dumb. He understood about half, but the half he understood was plenty. He felt like he was standing in a snowstorm.

"It's over la! Dammit!"

How to make an exit then? Fight? The Woman Warrior of National Salvation was skilled—setting all else aside, her mud-pellets were unendurable. That hunk was probably an evil monk from some temple or other. Even though Shi Zhaochang was studying swordsmanship, he still hadn't mastered Passing Though Earth, Water, Wood, and Metal. Master said he shouldn't try it until he had it down perfectly.

"Ah!" He said.

If this had only happened two days later he wouldn't have cared: in two days his discipleship would be over... So this was the end of it: he wouldn't even get the capital back on that fifty dollars.

"Not worth it all all..." he muttered.'

"Whaddya mean not worth it la? I sat on your lap twice la! That's twenty-seven minutes of sitting all together la. And I k'ed your iss five times la! How's that not worth fifty dollars la? And you saw one of my performances too la..."

"Well, I paid for the show," Shi Zhaochang said with a sigh, hurt. "And just now there's the rickshaw fare, eh? That was me."

"You got your money's worth la. You have to understand the market here la."

Shi Zhaochang couldn't speak. It was like his heart was being squeezed tight, and his lungs were being pressed. He wanted to leap up and beat some people, wanted to shatter the tables and chairs in the room to pieces. He had to scream wildly before he could be happy again.

But he couldn't move rashly.

But he could control his tone either.

"Evil! Evil!" His voice cracked. "Emperor Fumo in Heaven, I must... I must..."

"Eh? What's all this?!" The voice was clear and strong: The hunk. "Don't get yourself all cocky!" The guy brought up a fist. "Be smart, friend. You keep up this racket, and I'll, pow!"

"You you you!"

Suddenly—That hunk took a long stride toward Shi Zhaochang.

Suddenly—All the vigor in Shi Zhaochang's body went limp.

Oh, good Shi Zhaochang!—He had a plan. The specifics of his plan?—Turn around and run!

"Don't be taken in by them. Hehe. Thought I didn't know: You demon monk, you're all Evil. A hero doesn't fall for a trap he sees. Spending fifty dollars doesn't matter a bit—a hero spends money for the justice. Accounts will be settled later. In two days, I, Shi Zhaochang, must..."

He ran downstairs in one breath and bolted out the back door.

A gust of cold air. He closed his mouth and shivered hard.

12

The True Form of the Living Immortal

ALL THE LIGHTS WERE on in the room at the Shi house. The guest room was full of people. Everyone was chatting and picking their teeth. Everyone's faces were flushed. Everyone had just finished their meal: This, the author has just forgotten to relate. Honestly, the circumstances of the meal aren't worth going into in detail. The dear reader can well imagine it: For example, of course Mr. Liu Liu didn't eat much, just three bowls of thin dough noodle soup, five poached eggs, a little alcohol, some vegetables. In any case, he was planning on having fish porridge later that evening. Also, because Elder Mister Shi Boxiang was a junior classmate of Ancestor Lu, The Supreme Ultimate Master of course had to partake of that of the smoke and fire of the human realm, until even now his chin dripped with oil.

Mr. Liu Liu was carefully talking about the current situation: They were piling up sandbags and wire netting on XX Temple Street. It all looked quite serious.

"There will certainly be a battle. Last night, at Sean You

Zoo & Co..." *

"I heard the Chinese workers beat some kind of XX monk to death," Shi Boxiang wiped his few strands of beard with a napkin folded neatly into a rectangle, looking at this and that.

Elder Brother Disciple wanted to join in, but he was hiccupping something awful, causing him a lot of suffering, so he rubbed his belly and couldn't speak a word.

"Workers killed a monk?" Shi Zhaochang's eyes opened. His face was a little pale today.

Someone in a purple tie stood up, rubbed his hands and spoke to Shi Zhaochang in a lecturing voice:

"The workers were Chinese. The monks were XX monks. Toward this affair, our Campaign Against the Barbarians Fund Committee takes..."

"Who are the Evil ones and who are the Good ones?"

"What?" This brought the purple tie up short.

"I said... I said..." Shi Zhaochang licked his lips. "Monks believe in the bodhisattvas, which are Good of course. But... But... But... They're devils. Whose side should we take?"

"The Chinese, of course..."

But a tall man in western clothes patted him on the shoulder.

"What about those rooms in Zhabei?"

The purple tie didn't seem like he planned on continuing with Shi Zhaochang: He turned to the tall man, and started rubbing his hands enthusiastically:

"I don't encourage you to take those rooms in Zhabei. I fear there will be a battle in Zhabei. Moreover...I think Zhabei is

---

* Sean You Zoo & Co. 三友实业社—small factory in Zhabei. On Jan 18th, 1932, five Japanese monks were beaten. On the 19th, the factory was set on fire. This is seen as one of the final inciting events for open war.

too filthy. Zhabai's really not clean: that's the ethnic essence of the people in Zhabei. Zhabei'ers…"

"Ethnic essence?" The face of the tall man became severe. "Brother Liu Zhao, you take this ethnic essence too narrowly. Back in Guangdong, Teacher said to me personally…"

Suddenly a wild cry rang out:

"Ma! Ma!"

The sound of panicked feet.

Fourth Sister rushed into the guest room. Her left cheek was purple, and her face was covered in tears.

"What happened? What happened?" Mrs. Shi's face showed a couple of seconds of anxiety, then quickly calmed. "Ai, these children. Really, you're always…"

"Brother hit me."

"Zhaowu! Zhaowu! Ai, look. These children just infuriate me. All the time, hitting people. Usually, he means well. We have to remember this child Zhaowu will be fighting the XX next year. He's just practicing a bit now. But how could he go and hit Fourth Sister. There's no way Fourth Sister could win, isn't that right, hmm, Mrs Liu? That child Zhaowu, when he fights, he wins, but…but…Our eldest is stronger than he is. Our eldest practices every day, using gongfu against walls. Oh, it just kills me, even the walls have gone soft and beaten. Now the stove can't be lit in his room, the stove spits out smoke even up the wall, so it's better to just not light it."

She stopped for a while. She hesitated to mention this money-saving plan—it saved the price of the coal in the stove.

Shi Zhaochang felt an itch like a bug chewing on his heart. He did his best to keep happiness off his face, so he looked at everyone's expressions. He placed someone else's sentence in his belly:

"Even the walls have gone soft? Hm, that's powerful

gongfu!"

Or

"If Brother Zhaowu has such skill, what do we have to worry about the devils!"

But the other people didn't grasp the meaning of those words at all. Look at Master: Master was wiping the oil off his chin with the back of his hand. Elder Brother Disciple was hiccupping painfully.

Elder Brother Hu Genbao was watching Mrs. Shi, wrinkling up his entire face—he was laughing:

"There's no shortage of good fortune in your family: The two young masters in your family: Your family..."

Mrs. Shi quickly sighed:

"Our worries are true worries. I'm a person who does everything very earnestly. Everything—big or small—have to be earnest, don't you think so? Hmm Liu... Liu... Hmm... Mister Hu, don't you think? Mei Lanfang sings so well, that's because she's earnest. That day when we heard Mei Lanfang at the Kaiming the opera was so good, she sang... ah... what was it called? Boxiang do you recall, Boxiang?"

"Hm hm, eh?" The Elder Mister Shi Boxiang was dealing with Mr. Liu Liu, and rubbed his head when his wife called.

"I asked what Mei Lanfang sang that day?"

"What?"

"That day," Mrs. Shi's line of sight flittered from her husband's face and moved to Hu Genbao's sharp chin then lighted on the corners of Mrs. Liu's eyes. "We ran into so many people we know. Mr. Ma, you know, that man of Mrs. Ma's? Uhm, he was there. He's a fellow disciple under Ancestor Lu, he's a classmate of Boxiang. Ancestor Lu loved the two of them most. Ancestor Lu said that our house... That people like us had native... native something or other..."

This was a specific term, but she couldn't remember it. She paused for a bit, lightly rubbing her temple and checking to make sure her hair covered that purple scar. Then she propped herself up on the sofa with her right hand as if she were going to continue speaking, but she couldn't find her conversation partner. Hu Genbao and Shi Zhaochang were grunting toward "second brother" to talk. Mrs. Liu noticed that Mr. Liu Liu was talking with Elder Mister Shi Boxiang.

Mr. Liu Liu patted his chest and asked if Elder Mister Shi would be moving. If a battle really broke out, it wouldn't be a joke.

"If they start fighting, you would be in a real mess here."

"Yes," Elder Mister Shi Boxiang frowned in worry.

"So you should escape over to my place for the moment. You could use our second and third floor garret rooms. What do you think?"

At this, he glanced at Mrs. Liu. Mrs. Liu was paying all her attention to Elder Mister Shi's expression. Elder Mister Shi wiped his beard with a handkerchief. A little ill at ease, he asked:

"You're certain they'll fight?"

"Of course." A raised eyebrow. "Houses in the French Concession are already full. Everyone probably already knows this area is untenable and have all moved into the French Concession. Looking at you... I think you had better live at my place first, then we can gradually move your things."

Mrs. Liu stood up and moved to Shi Boxiang with a giggle.

"It's best this way. It's best this way, cram yourselves into the two little rooms first and we'll deal with the rest later. The good thing is rent is cheap: only... only... for the two rooms, it's only one hundred forty *liang*."

He rubbed his beard.

Mr. Liu Liu looked forcefully at Mrs. Liu while he skillfully cracked a rose-roasted pumpkin seed.

His mouth was busy for this moment: getting the meat of the seed out and chewing, spitting out the shell, and using his tongue to speak. His voice was vaguely slurred as if he were drunk.

"The Campaign Against the Barbarian Fund Committee will... In the future will buy a spot..." snap... snap... "On Edward VII Avenue or Bubbling Well Road, they'll buy..." Ptoo! "Build a seven story building..." snap... snap... "This plan... plan..." Crack! "Still need to add some subordinate organizations, like..." ptoo!

The Elder Mister Shi Boxiang, seemingly worried that he might get a seed shell spat on his face, lightly wrinkled his brows. He took advantage of Mr. Liu Liu going back for more seeds to ask, almost to himself:

"But will they actually fight?"

"That's certain!" Mr. Liu Liu was taking more seeds while answering—his hand hovered over the seed plate. "The Supreme Ultimate Master can see the future, ask..." A pause. "Supreme Ultimate Master..." crack! "In the end, will war..." Ptoo! "Will this..."

One after another, several pairs of eyes settled on The Supreme Ultimate Master.

The Supreme Ultimate Master smiled: A line of white in between two golden teeth.

"The XX devils are..." His oily hands massaged his eyes, a gob of rheum stuck to his finger.

Shi Zhaochang looked at everyone's faces. Everyone was earnestly awaiting The Supreme Ultimate Master's next words. Only Elder Brother Disciple was just rubbing his belly and wiping his head, hiccupping with great effort.

"Hic!... Hic!..." It couldn't wait for The Supreme Ultimate Master's next words. This perfected man just shrugged so deep that even his ears were lost in his shoulders.

Hu Genbao looked at The Supreme Ultimate Master, and then smiled at the Elder Mister Shi Boxiang.

"Master is... Master is... You understand these things: there are many things that are inconvenient to speak of. Master simply... This is the sort of thing that cannot be divulged. Uh..."

"This is a heavenly secret."

"Ah, ah." Nodding heads.

"However... However..." Mrs. Shi broke in loudly in a sharper voice than usual. "However, there is native... native... For some types of people, it's alright. To people with native... What is that native-whatever. Boxiang, what's it called, native-whatsit?"

"Native ability?"

"Ah, ah, ah, Native ability. Heavenly secrets can be told to those with native ability, isn't that so? What do you say, ah, Supreme, uh.. Master... Master... Uncle Master?"

Uncle Master nodded.

Naturally, those with native ability can be..."

"Right! Didn't I say it? Native ability is innate in people... People with native ability—there's an aura around the top of the head, you can see it when the lights are turned off. That aura..."

The Supreme Ultimate Master let his shoulders droop back from his shrug, and forced his head upward. But you still couldn't see his neck. On his face was a smile as serene as a bodhisattva.

"Not necessarily. Only the living immortals—they emit the purple aura from their heads. Also you can see the living immortal's previous incarnation is, the true form of the living immortal…"

Suddenly a man stood up in the corner of the room and waved his arms to try to get everyone to quiet down. Then he gave a proposal in formal Mandarin:

He asked The Supreme Ultimate Master to emit a bit of that purple light for everyone to see, that way they could know "the aforementioned" perfected man… I'm sorry, this man who made the proposal used the word "the aforementioned" only because he had been a secretary. His meaning: Only to see the true form of the living immortal.

Everyone applauded. Everyone's gaze fell on the sallow face of The Supreme Ultimate Master. The Supreme Ultimate Master's sallow face flushed red as he stuttered.

"I…I…Today, I partook of alcohol, I… it can only be done with the utmost focus…"

But the Elder Mister Shi Boxiang beseeched him with arms clasped in salute. Liu Zhao also adjusted his purple tie and made a formal bow.

"We entreat you…"

Everyone looked on with sincere faces. Everyone excitedly awaited the true form of the living immortal.

The living immortal smiled to his cheeks and forced out, "This… this… only children can actually see it. Adults are…"

"Zhaowu! Zhaowu!" Mrs. Shi shouted with enough force to rock her head back, then she immediately rocked back so her hair would fall to cover her temple.

Drat. The Supreme Ultimate Master right then had forgotten there were children in the house. But he did remember that Zhaowu was sixteen: Wasn't he going to be a division commander?

He relaxed and said, "Only those who have not passed

sixteen can see it…"

"Our Zhaowu is just fifteen."

"But… But…"

"If fifteen is still too old, we've got younger here too."

The Elder Mister Shi Boxiang glanced over to Fourth Sister who had just come sobbing into the guest room.

Fourth Sister had clambered over next a side table eating candy from a plate—the candy and tears mixing together on her face.

The Supreme Ultimate Master sighed.

At the door appeared Shi Zhaowu, with that rotten-buddha-hand-melon head of his and his mouth that pushed the gums outside.

"Hehe!"

"Sit down!" softly said. "Watch the true form of The Supreme Ultimate Master."

The atmosphere in the room became more serious.

Everyone sat quietly, even breathing silently. Fourth Sister stood by her mother. Mr. Liu Liu put the seeds in his hands down on the table. Half Mote covered his mouth with his hand. Shi Zhaowu didn't dare smile, just setting his pair of goldfish eyes on The Supreme Ultimate Master. Shi Zhaochang stood on tiptoe to turn off the light.

"I'll give it a try," The Supreme Ultimate Master said shakily. "But today I have partaken of alcohol, I'm afraid that… I'm afraid it won't be like usual… I'm afraid it will be weak… For good or ill, please, everyone…"

Darkness. Silence.

The sound of the pendulum. The horn of a car outside. A hiccup broke forth from Half Mote's throat sharply.

"Hic!"

One minute. Two minutes. Three minutes.

Elder Mister Shi Boxiang's voice asked Shi Zhaowu:

"Do you see anything?"

The fifteen-year-old boy cried out:

"I see it!"

Everyone was stunned.

"What do you see?"

"I see a great big turtle!"

"Ha!"

"I'm not tricking you. If I'm lying, I'm a dog fucker."

"I also see a big turtle," Fourth Sister clapped.

Silence.

Mrs. Shi said lightly, "Zhaowu, do you see the purple light?"

"I see a dog dick coming out of his head!"

"Don't talk nonsense."

"If I'm talking nonsense, I'm a motherfucker."

"I see a… see a… a…" Fourth Sister blurted out, forgetting what her brother said he saw.

Silence.

"I see a stupid dupe, how about you?" Shi Zhaowu casually asked his sister.

"I see a stupid dupe, too."

"I see a pig-family beggar bumpkin stupid."

"I see… I see…"

"Hehe, too hard for you? I see…"

Suddenly a flash in the room stabbed at everyone's eyes.

The Elder Mister Shi Boxiang's right hand slowly came away from the switch and went back into his pocket.

The Supreme Ultimate Master's face had gone green.

Shi Zhaochang's face flushed, he bit his lip, and glared at Shi Zhaowu. Shi Zhaowu was still talking to Fourth Sister: He talked and talked and then—Pow! He rushed up and slapped her across the mouth, then grabbed her by the hair and dragged her out of the room.

Fourth Sister cried out sharply. Shi Zhaowu cursed at her. Mistress Shi shouted and chased after them. Mrs. Liu roared off to help. And old servant woman bundled Fourth Sister away from Mrs. Liu. The wailing trailed off far away with the sound of her footsteps. A crash of a slammed door cut off the noise.

Mrs. Liu sighed and looked at the guest room. She thought to ask Mistress Shi if they would move after all, but she opened her mouth without speaking. She didn't return to the guest room. She stood agape for a few minutes and then went upstairs.

"So The Supreme Ultimate Master was a disciple of Ancestor Lu?" She asked, apropos of nothing.

Mistress Shi rubbed her hair, replying as noted below:

"He is of the same generation as Ancestor Lu. Boxiang is a disciple of Ancestor Lu, he went often to kowtow to him. It was just kowtowing, then he would head home and do other things. He always handled things very very carefully. In the past, he handled things at the yamen a bit too carefully, he did things... Ah. Hmph. Busy from day to night. And I had to help take care of public affairs, too. Mrs Liu, help me think this through... I work so hard that I end up like this. I'm simply so busy I'm going to die. Oh don't bother yourself! Let me turn on the lights, or else you'll trip. Be careful Mrs. Liu. In all things you have to be careful. Of course, I'm not at a loss when looking at public affairs. I have to handle the affairs of the house, think about that. Boxiang says, "You're too busy, I should get a concubine! She could help you out. What do you think?" So infuriating, he wants a concubine? Why would he have cause to resent me—and he wants a concubine. I'd like to ask him, "You old fart, what have I done to you? I've raised son for you and his horoscope is certainly a good one. I've managed the house for you, and I've suffered so much for that. If you resent me for not being pretty, well then I ask you, What of me is ugly? Are my eyes no good? My nose bad? My skin too coarse? My hands aren't good? Mouth? Is my figure poor?... I'm not too bad for you." What do you think Mrs. Liu? Isn't that so? I say it has to be all stirred up by that eldest of mine. Our eldest young master isn't so bad at provoking things. Hmph. For a person like that to go out as a warrior, and to go fight the XX devils! He'd never be a division commander. How can he fight the foreigners without soldiers? Isn't that so, uh, Mrs. Liu. And he's got mixed up with a woman, Zhaowu said they..."

And so on. Because when Mistress Shi got to that point in her speech, she went into the washroom with Mrs. Liu and they closed the door.

13

Thirteenth Sister

IT SEEMS THAT the situation was getting worse every day.

Mr. Liu Liu and Mrs. Liu went to the Shi house almost every day to urge them to move to the French Concession. Mistress Shi thought that the garret rooms were too expensive, and wanted to look for another house, but she couldn't find one whatever she did.

On seeing all of the neighbors loading up car after car of luggage and boxes, driving off south on North Sichuan Road, the Elder Master Shi Boxiang lost his temper.

"What will we do if we can't find a house?"

If they really do start fighting here, it won't be any laughing matter. This building is too close to the XX headquarters.

"We'll just go to the Liu's for a few days."

But Shi Zhaochang refused to go.

"You go. I won't go."

Shi Zhaochang had just finished his lessons the previous day. He learned how to spit blades, learned the divination of the Marvelous Gate and Shrouded Prime. He could also...

"That's dangerous," his father said, but his tone wasn't that severe.

The corners of Shi Zhaochang's mouth curved down, and he took a splayfooted stride forward, his right thumb stuck out.

"A real hero can attain merit here. If fighting breaks out here... All the better. If after a few days nothing happens, I'll have to go beyond the northern pass."

"The northern pass?"

"Hmph!" A great echoing sound came from his nose.

Mistress Shi sighed quietly.

"I absolutely won't go, but then again what can we do? Ah, the rooms over there are too small…"

Accordingly, she gathered up her luggage: powder, rouge, rose-roasted pumpkin seeds, leather shoes, Crème Simon, these things filled up three baskets. But the mahjong set wouldn't fit, so it was stuffed into Elder Master Shi's clothing bag so that he had to pack one fewer silk jacket, otherwise the mahjong set wouldn't fit. Of course the furniture wouldn't go, that would have to wait until they found a house. Right, there was one other thing.

"Oh, we need to leave someone here to watch over the house."

Shi Zhaochang appointed Little Wang. Little Wang was the one he had subdued.

"I want Little Wang to stay here."

"But… But…" Mistress Shi was worried that the cook at the Liu's would only be able to make dough noodle soup. They could never get used to that.

"Fine," Elder Master Shi said. "We'll leave Little Wang here."

Zhaochang figured he had everything settled, so he could go take care of his things.

"Have to get it done quickly," He rushed out the door.

His heart was pounding. He couldn't say how his luck would run this time. But he had to be fast. If the devils started the fight he wouldn't have the time for this.

His hands were in his sleeves, eyes focused on his splayfoot stance. He puffed out a breath. If he couldn't take care of this in the next day or two...

"All things must rely on fate. Master said..."

Oh, Master said he was a man of fate.

A smile flashed from the corners of his mouth, and his heart pounded even harder.

"Ah, I'll find her today. How could such a big place as Shanghai be without a Thirteenth Sister?"

Oh, it turns out he is looking for a Thirteenth Sister!

That's right! Looking for a Thirteenth Sister. Elder Brother said there were a lot of those kind of people at the Southern Market, so today Elder Brother is going with him to look. But, he has to spend a bit of money. Right now that fated Thirteenth Sister is waiting there.

Faster dammit. He called for a rickshaw.

"Rick..." but then he remembered Shanghainese called out "Dicksaw." "Dick..."

Right then he thought of something else. He spun around and darted into his house, and in one breath made it up to his room.

His room was just as cold as it was outside. The window latch had never been fixed, so the paper in the window rattled. The stove hadn't been lit in a week, but there was still a big pile of soot in the stove tray. The Yue Fei in the poster on the wall seemed to fear the cold a bit—his belly didn't stick out as much.

Shi Zhaochang leapt over to his bed and lifted up the mattress to pull out the brocade box.

"Dammit!" Shi Zhaochang pulled out the mud-pellet from the box. He raised his arm to throw the mud-pellet out the window, but one of the women was drying her underthings on the opposite balcony. He lowered his arm. His gongfu was strong now, and he didn't want to accidentally kill her with it.

He looked all around, then threw the mud-pellet in the spittoon.

Just like that, there was nothing at all between him and the Woman Warrior of National Salvation, Miss He Manli.

"Evil!" he said between clenched teeth. But then he sighed.

He felt she must be Evil long ago, but only recently could he do it: could he break it off. To lose a woman like that didn't mean anything. He could never do good deeds with anyone who was Evil, isn't that right.

"Men and women mixed up together, look at the Evil energy!"

He always thought that. He even let it slip when he was walking with Elder Brother. Elder Brother said something to him, he said...

"Eh? Uh?"

This all might have just been someone conjured by The Supreme Ultimate Master to test his disciple's heart. Perhaps the Woman Warrior of National Salvation was the incarnation of some monster come to harm Shi Zhaochang.

But, when he thought about that woman warrior, his heart would ache. How? Did he love her? That he couldn't admit. Maybe he regretted spending fifty dollars all for nothing. Also, he was always recalling that energy when she sat on his lap, the energy of the two of them, lip to lip. It was like an aftertaste of a dream on waking.

He quietly breathed out through his teeth. He wouldn't let Elder Brother know, otherwise Elder Brother would take him for someone who is pining for an Evil woman.

Sitting on his lap...

But there was also that hunk sitting on her lap!

"Humph!" The tendon in Shi Zhaochang's cheek popped out. "Evil!"

He started walking a bit faster.

"Second Brother, slow down," Hu Genbao caught up to him. "It's still early."

Shi Zhaochang smiled apologetically, then fell back to his original gait.

"I'm... I'm... I'm worried that if we are late, we won't find her."

This time he must find a true woman warrior. A true Thirteenth Sister. One who is Good, without any doubt.

"Good. Good. Good." He recited to himself. "Not like the Woman Warrior of National Salvation, with her... Men and women all mixed up together. Not like the way she..."

Then a thought popped into his head—like a wedge painfully poking into his heart. It was like he had caught a fever. His lips trembled. He feared he had accidently spoken aloud. He stole a glance at Hu Genbao.

"Surely I'm not Evil, oh!"

The Evil of woman and men mixed up together, but Shi Zhaochang had to find a Thirteenth Sister, that couldn't be also...? There wouldn't be anything mixed up about it, but to have no wariness at all between man and woman...

It was that last that was difficult to take.

"Elder Brother," he panted out, "You said... You said...You said..."

He stuttered along for a long time before coming out with the question of whether or not a man like him going and looking for a Thirteenth Sister to be with might be not proper.

"Second Brother, don't worry. If it weren't proper, would your Elder Brother be going with you?"

Shi Zhaochang smiled and exhaled. He had to restrain himself from embracing Elder Brother.

The world today is truly not like it was in the past: A

certain cause would lead to a certain result. The Thirteenth Sister of the past had a relationship with Lord An. And this was ordained by heaven as well. Master had said that there was a fated connection between him and a woman warrior. He and that woman warrior would do good deeds, assisted by Elder Brother and Elder Brother Disciple. He also had to subdue those Evil ones, He Manli and that Missed-Whatever-Tao. He had to get back the capital that he laid out. But this would have to wait until he vanquished the devils. First, he would go to…

Elder Brother pulled at his arm.

"Second Brother, we're here. Here it is!"

There was an empty space surrounded by some people. In the center was a sallow-faced guy stripped to the waist.

He shouted out, "At home one relies on parents, but once you leave the home you must rely on friends… Ka-ching! Ka-ching!"

The surrounding people tossed in some copper coins. They fell into the muddy earth with a plopping sound.

Shi Zhaochang did not throw anything. First he had to see Thirteenth Sister, otherwise it would be a waste of copper and wouldn't be worth it.

He pushed through the crowd. An awful smell assaulted his nose. These people seemed to all be rickshaw pullers or baggage haulers. But Shi Zhaochang persisted, because Elder Brother was pushing him.

"There, Elder Brother, look."

A girl! Probably fifteen years old. Her face was shiny and pallid, and skinny as a dried fish. Her thick cotton-padded jacket had faded green cotton poking out of several holes. A black belt cinched up tight making her whole body look like a fish bladder. Cotton pants ran below into leg wraps.

This girl had her braids in her mouth as she looked lethargically at the sallow-faced man.

"...the Overturned Tripod!..." The man shouted. "A man can make a slip, a horse can throw a shoe. Practice good or practice vice, I hope I can rely on you..."

The girl spat into her hands and put her hands on the ground as her legs shot up straight to the sky.

Her feet were bound like dumplings.

Ah, truly it was Thirteenth Sister!

Then she stuck her right hand into the air as her body shifted to the left and her leg stuck out to the right.

The sallow-faced man shouted out, "There it is! Drawing the bow from the left and the right!"

The girl put her left hand up into the air again.

Shi Zhaochang tried to think what he should do. So he loudly shouted out, "Bravo!"

The sallow-faced man locked eyes with him.

Thirteenth Sister stood back up panting, letting her braid out of her mouth and wiping the sweat from her brow with her sleeve.

"How?..." Shi Zhaochang stared carefully at her. "Elder Brother, is Thirteenth Sister like that?"

Elder Brother stuck his chest back and aimed his sharp face at Shi Zhaochang, then hesitated. His face broke out all over wrinkled in smiles.

"Not to your fancy? There's only one in Shanghai. This one right here. There's no other shop for it. Second Brother you are... You are... Master said that you and she are fated."

For some reason Shi Zhaochang's heart thumped and his face flushed.

"Fine," he muttered. This Thirteenth Sister wasn't horrible, she was just a little dirty. If you stripped her and scrubbed her...you'd have to scrub, might suffer some damage to the vital essence. And this Thirteenth Sister was much cheaper than the Woman Warrior of National Salvation.

His entire body felt warm. He stared attentively at Thirteenth Sister until the crowd started to break up.

The sallow-faced man picked his padded jacket from the ground and put it right on his shiny torso—no undergarment at all. Then he grumbled something at the guy who played the drums as he collected his things.

Shi Zhaochang watched Thirteenth Sister

Thirteenth Sister took off her belt, hocked a clump of yellow snot on the muddy ground, and rubbed her palms together.

Shi Zhaochang tilted his head to glance at Elder Brother, who stuck out his chin in encouragement. And so he quite cautiously took up his Upright stance and slowly walked toward Thirteenth Sister. His breath started to come quickly. He took a deep breath and saluted Thirteenth Sister. His tongue moved like it was twitching.

"I...I...I, Shi Zhaochang... You're gongfu is so good...Here is... Here is twenty cents..."

Thirteenth Sister seemed to become stone, staring at him without moving a muscle.

He reached into his pocket where there were five "Guangdong Double Dimes." He didn't know which ones were the lead ones. But he had to pull his hand out quickly.

Ah, who the hell cares, just grab whichever.

"Uh, here it is," he moved closer to Thirteenth Sister and the sallow-faced man turned around to look at him carefully, but he didn't notice. "I... I have to fight the XX devils with you. Together we... we also will suppress the bandits, we... we... There are people in this world who don't know their place, they don't believe in the Divine Way... Not like... We have to subdue them… Then we have to subdue the Woman Warrior of National Salvation… Evil…"

The girl's eyes were wide open, looking at his hands, then his face. She didn't take the twenty cents. He lifted up his right hand, fingers trembling.

Ah, she thinks it's too little. He determinedly thrust his hand back in his pocket.

"Another twenty cents… We are connected by fate…"

But Thirteenth Sister took two steps backward, turning her head to look for the sallow-faced man.

There was a sudden clash of noise as he threw a gong on the drums. Then he advanced on Shi Zhaochang.

"Getting' fresh with me girl, eh!" He locked eyes as he spoke, spitting in his hands.

Shi Zhaochang trembled all over, politely bending at the waist. His eyes were on him, but then he shot a glance at Thirteenth Sister. "I, I… The Supreme Ultimate Master is my Master, I am… I am Shi Zhaochang… I can spit blades and pass though earth, water, wood, and metal…"

This sputtered from the mouth of the other man:

"Aye know do not* me girl… You… Your grannie's cock!"

Thwack! Shi Zhaochang was cracked in the face.

"What! You! You!" Shi Zhaochang didn't have time to get into his stance, he stumbled to the side.

Next he took a punch to the chest: Bam! There was a whiff of Shaolin style in it.

Shi Zhaochang retreated a couple of steps and took stock of his opponent. He turned his head to look for Elder Brother. Who knows where he had run off to.

---

* In the original: "Note: Mr. Typesetter, this is not a mistake. Please do not correct this to "do not know.""

The sallow-faced man stood there with clenched fists for a while, eyeing Shi Zhaochang before tottering off to leave.

"Get lost!" He picked up his load.

Shi Zhaochang's right hand dropped the two Guangdong Double Dimes in his pocket with a clink. He looked at the silhouette of the sallow-faced man shouldering his load, and resolved to have a go at him—test their skill. In a flash, his legs formed a stance: and he held the stance for three minutes, four minutes, five minutes, all without moving a muscle.

What?

The others had long gone.

"Come here!" Shi Zhaochang yelled.

But no one heard him.

After he held the stance for a while, once his legs were sore and trembling he finally gradually stood up straight. Then he shielded his eyes with his right hand and looked all around. He sighed and started to walk. His chest hurt a little bit and his right cheek felt as hot as if it had been scalded.

"Whose fault is this?" Another sigh, and his heart pounded nearly out of his chest.

Thirteenth Sister's guard in terms of gender mixing was even more Proper than Shi Zhaochang's. He stuck this in his mind and thought about it. He analyzed himself—had he been tainted by the Evil spirit of the Warrior Woman of National Salvation? The entire journey he was as if in a dream.

"This is it, isn't it?" He knelt facing the window. "Hear me Emperor Guan: I, Shi Zhaochang…"

He got on his bed but couldn't sleep. He planned to go back tomorrow and offer his apology to Thirteenth Sister.

"I've been tainted by this New School—and that's Evil. I'm like…" He said this to himself, but looked around like someone might have heard him.

Don't worry: The family had moved to the house of Mr. Liu Liu. In the whole building was only himself and Little Wang. All was quiet.

Tomorrow he would go looking for Thirteenth Sister, Elder Brother and Elder Brother Disciple would help them out as they did good deeds. Spending a few dozen cents wouldn't matter. He needed to bring a sword...

Suddenly-

Bang! Bang bang! Bang bang bang bang bang!

Gunshots!

"What's this!"

14

Flying Blades Kill the Enemy

LITTLE WANG RUSHED into Shi Zhaochang's room.
"Elder Master, we're done for! This is bad!"

There was no light in the room.

Shi Zhaochang lifted his quilt and sat up, pulling on his silk jacket. His teeth were disobediently chattering the whole time like an electric bell. His lips had gone white. Afraid? Who's afraid! It was bitterly cold, that's all.

"Don't rush," Shi Zhaochang's voice quavered.

The sounds of gunshots outside were coming closer together. It sounded like there was some trouble nearby. It was like the bang bang of the gunshots were happening right outside the window, shaking so much that his heart hurt.

Little Wang shrieked out in falsetto: "Elder Master, Elder Master, we have to leave now!"

"Leave!" Shi Zhaochang go back on the bed, his legs were fighting to keep him from standing up. "Little Wang, we must do good deeds… Buy me a stealth suit…"

"What?!"

He gritted his teeth and calmly said, "Stealth. Suit. Warriors wear them."

"Where would I go to buy that? Master! Don't… don't…"

"How? You!" Shi Zhaochang bared his teeth at Little Wang as if he were going to eat him up. "Did I, Elder Master Shi, not subdue you? Didn't you cast aside Evil and return to the path of Good! Don't rush, we must fight the XX devils… My

Elder Brother and Elder Brother Disciple will come to assist me. Wait a bit, they must come, and we must… must, must…"

But the other didn't pay any attention to this—that low born nothing!

"Don't… Don't… Master, let's go downstairs and lie down on the floor. Don't be so… so…"

Little Wang turned and fled.

Reddish clouds smeared across the sky outside the window, sometimes darker, sometimes lighter.

The gunshots came so thick the sounded as one—the cracks and bangs couldn't be distinguished, like peals of thunder crying out unending.

Someone was calling out something indistinctly.

"Little Wang! Little Wang!" Shi Zhaochang rushed out the door after him. In the darkness, with only the light of the fires, he came across a vague shadow.

Little Wang on the floor of the guest room.

The gunshots come without a letup: Pow! Pow! Pow! Just like they were flying through inside the room. The further-away shots sounded a bit like birds: "tweee!"

"Quickly Master, get down, quickly…"

"Little Wang, hurry and go buy me a stealth suit. I must…"

"I won't go! I won't go! The guns…. I'm afraid I'll catch a bullet… You… You…"

"You attend me. When I tell you to do something…"

"I won't go! I won't go! I'd rather… rather…"

Suddenly the heavens cried out with booms—one after another so that people's heads would swell.

Airplanes!

Things got worse and worse. Dammit, he needed that stealth suit now! "Little Wang! Little Wang…"

"I won't go! I won't go! Take this money, you can order me

however you like but I won't do it, I... I..."

Then for some reason, Little Wang began to cry, oh!

Boom!

Crash! The glass in the window shattered.

The house shuddered. All the vases and decorations all fell off to the ground. The silver plate someone had given to the Elder Master Shi Boxiang tumbled with a flip, its glass case shattering into thousands of pieces.

Little Wang cried out with a sharp mad shout and rolled under the sofa. Panting and crying, he yelled, "It's all over this time, but... but... mother!"

The electric lights went out.

Shi Zhaochang's legs went weak, and he sat down on the floor.

A column of black smoke rose in the flame-red sky. Amid the sounds of gunfire were the sounds of collapsing buildings like the rolling of the tide.

The airplanes screamed with more and more intensity, like they were flying inside the room, and the floor rocked and trembled.

"Ah!" Little Wang cried out sharply, darted out from under the sofa and ran outside.

Shi Zhaochang jumped up to hold him back.

"Little Wang, you can't go! Buy the stealth suit... My Elder Brother and the rest will be here soon... We will do good deeds..."

"I can't, I..."

"Little Wang, didn't you swear obedience to me? You have to obey me. I gave you twenty cents, twenty... not lead coins, you..."

"I, I, I..."

"Don't go, Little Wang, and you... I, your Elder Young

Master will give you another twenty cents!"

But Little Wang twisted his body and fled.

The sound of airplanes went further away. Then there was one more: "Boom!"

"I must prepare the talisman!" Shi Zhaochang ran into his room.

Prepare the talisman and wait for Elder Brother and Elder Brother Disciple to come, then they could go and fight the devils together. If only he had the time to look for Thirteenth Sister.

He pulled a paper box from a drawer. Inside were twenty or thirty Golden Pills. His Master gave this to him.

"Disciple, these Golden Pills were refined by I, The Supreme Ultimate Master and Xuan Nü of the Nine Heavens. Once disciple eats one, damned all if he don't need fear no flood, fire or blade. If someone breathes his last, this Golden Pill can bring him back to life."

It was that kind of thing.

Shi Zhaochang stuffed one of the pills into his mouth. Soft, sweet, and it had a kind of banana flavor.

The sound of gunshots eased a bit, the sounds was cut by someone screaming. Then there was a sudden sound like someone striking a wooden fish that made the house jump: Bambambambambambambam...

From near and far away was: Bang! Bang! Bang!

Shi Zhaochang grit his teeth, not at all afraid. He just shivered and his shoulders twitched, then he slowly hunted for the sword his master gave him. It was very small, drawn from the scabbard it wasn't even half a foot long. He struck a match to see if he wasn't mistaken.

With the match lit, we can see the foreign words carved on the blade:

"G.H. PENKNIFE CO. SHANGHAI"

There was a red thread wound around the hilt.

"Ah, no mistake." Shi Zhaochang put it and the box of Golden Pills in his pocket.

"What to do? He had to wait for Elder Brother and Elder Brother Disciple. Looking around, he shivered again. If he were to go out to win honor all by himself, that would be showing a lack of respect to the two of them, and to Master.

He lacked a stealth suit, too. The one he had was stretched out and ripped to the point of being useless. To wear torn up clothes would be too demeaning.

He also lacked a Thirteenth Sister.

He shuddered and sighed. Perhaps The Supreme Ultimate Master would be struck with a flash of insight and make a divination that would show he must have Elder Brother and Elder Brother Disciple send Thirteenth Sister, and bring along a stealth suit too. He must go, hand in hand with Thirteenth Sister…

Bang!

BAM!

Shi Zhaochang was so startled he nearly fell over. He didn't have time to get into his upright stance, he just shot out the doorway. It seemed like he worried someone might come rushing up. He hesitated behind the door to the guest room. But after five or six minutes, he remembered the Golden Pill he had swallowed.

"Haha! I don't fear you!" He strode out in his upright stance.

Right then someone bolted out and ran right into Shi Zhaochang.

"Who?!"

"It's me." Little Wang.

"How?"

"I couldn't get out." Little Wang hid on the sofa, trembling so much that the sofa springs squeaked.

Boom—Crash!

The house shook like it was about to collapse.

"I'm not afraid!" Shi Zhaochang spat out through gritted teeth. "Follow me and those shells and bombs won't do a thing to you. I need to... need to..."

But he still wouldn't leave. He had to wait from Elder Brother and Elder Brother Disciple to bring Thirteenth Sister.

But no one ever came.

His eyeballs were getting dry. His upper eyelids were coming down like hammers. No matter what gongfu he tried he couldn't keep them up. For several nights he hadn't slept. That day Liu Zhao tried to get him to make a donation, he was up the whole night with worry. Then falling out with the Woman Warrior of National Salvation had him up all night with anger. After offending Thirteenth Sister, he was up thinking the entire night. Now he was just...

His butt hit the sofa.

Little Wang jumped up in fright, but then after five or six minutes burrowed back down.

Outside, the gunshots went thick and then sparse. Not long after there was the rolling scraping sound all mixed together: Bang! Bang! Bang!

Shi Zhaochang closed his eyes. He felt his body floating up. He seemed to see a bullet come from the muzzle of a rifle soaring wildly through the streets. Then there was some black thing in front of him: ah, it was someone fleeing for their life. He wanted to tell them not to worry, but he couldn't make any sound.

The fleeing silhouette gradually started to glow and became a multicolored body. The face appeared: Ah! The Woman

Warrior of National Salvation!

"Let her suffer a little bit."

"Great hero! Quick come save me la!" Her face was streaked with tears.

"You are Evil. You, you… There are still fifty dollars of mine in your…"

"I've cast aside Evil and turned to the Good la," the Woman Warrior raised her hand for him to see. In her hand was a head—the head of that Missed-Whatever Tao.

"You, you…you…"

Then the Woman Warrior of National Salvation sat down on him lap and snuggled her head against him. He smelled her scent of sandalwood and sardine oil. Next to him sat Elder Brother and Elder Brother Disciple.

"Second Brother, Master has arrived," Elder Brother stood perfectly as one should.

Master sat on a cloud dais, rubbing his red eyes with his fingers.

"Disciple, go forth now and win honor. Many are waiting for you to kill the devils."

"Your disciple will go immediately," He jumped up and ran outside.

But in front of him he was blocked by people kneeling in a circle around him: Mr. Liu Liu, Mrs. Liu, Liu Zhao, Shi Zhaowu, Mistress Shi.

"Brother Shi Wuchang," Liu Zhao kowtowed. "You must save the people. You see how so many people await your… Save us, we won't ask you to make a donation…"

Oh, right, behind him, knelt uncountable millions of regular people.

"Very well. I will go… Little Wang, bring me my stealth suit!"

Elder Master Shi Boxiang appeared before him, stroking Shi Zhaochang's head.

"Only now do I realize you have such ability. Only if you go out on a campaign will the evildoers of the world be wiped out, only then with the world be at peace. Zhaowu has no real future. You can win honor and save so much money. I spent so much money raising you—the return on investment is incredible."

"Father, only now do you understand…"

But father wasn't father: it was Thirteenth Sister.

The Woman Warrior for National Salvation appeared on his shoulder smoking a cigarette, telling him she loved him, and he didn't need to spend a cent. He said nothing, just puffed out her cheeks, sniffed, and ran out.

On the firing line!

"I, Shi Zhaochang, have arrived!"

The guns fired off wildly, but whenever a bullet was fired toward him, it would turn away.

"Watch my blade!" He took out the blade in his hand.

The devil soldiers fell to the ground like a collapsing wall.

His blade flew everywhere, and one after another, heads rolled to the ground. He had to kill all of the evildoers: Those who don't believe in the Divine Way, that don't know their places, that mixed men and women together. And also those two guys who tried to get donations at the door to the theatre. And the rickshaw pullers that wouldn't take the lead dimes.

Somehow he killed all the way into the nation of the devils. Their emperor's face was made up like the 'painted face' in an opera, and a pheasant feather stuck out from the top of his head. They all kneeled before him.

"Great warrior, spare us, great warrior…"

"Do you submit to me, Shi Zhaochang?"

"You servant is...

The suddenly from all over, millions upon millions cried out: "Long live Shi Zhaochang! Long Live Shi Zhaochang!"

But was Shi Zhaochang a bit unhappy? How dare they address him by shouting out his personal name?

There was a sound like firecrackers outside.

Firecrackers came flying in next to his ears. He jumped.

"Ah!"

He was still on the sofa in the guest room.

It was light. There was a grayish light slanting in from the window.

Elder Brother and Elder Brother Disciple hadn't come. Thirteenth Sister didn't come. There was only him and Little Wang here. Little Wang was sleeping on the floor face up, with sticky saliva seeping out of the corners of his mouth, flowing down his cheeks, and snorts came from his nose.

All around was quiet, with only the occasional gunshot or two.

"They still haven't come," Shi Zhaochang muttered with a yawn.

If only they would come, his dream would be put into action.

His legs were numb, and when he stood, he nearly tripped.

"I'll take a look outside."

As soon as the door opened a chill came in. He shivered.

The alley seemed to be a deserted world. He could only see a couple of people with bundles on their backs running off. He groused Elder Brother and Elder Brother Disciple hadn't come, otherwise—those refugees would have been saved long ago. But how many lives were wronged over night!

It is all preordained, ah!

But...

"If they don't come by tomorrow, then I'll have to…"

Then he would have to go out and win honor by himself.

But his legs didn't have any strength, his teeth chattered, shaking so much that his cheeks shook. His heart raced one moment and then calmed the next. He forced himself to calm down, but it didn't do any good at all. A thought came to him that maybe this feeling was what is called the "Flash of Insight."

"It's been this flash of insight, dammit!"

Maybe Elder Brother and Elder Brother Disciple were about to arrive. Maybe Thirteenth Sister was in trouble.

He blew out a breath. This "Flash of Insight" was a little tough to take.

"I'll go save Thirteenth Sister," he muttered.

He legs went weak and he leaned against the wall. His hand rubbed his forehead—he was burning up.

"I'm hungry. I'll have Little Wang order a bowl of dough noodle soup …"

He leaned against the wall, unmoving. He hoped that Little Wang would have a flash of insight too, and figure out that his master's stomach was empty so that he would order some dough noodle soup and the rest.

Little Wang did really have a flash of insight. Little Wang ran out.

"Master, it's time to hurry… quickly, master. We have to leave now!"

"I won't leave. I have to fight the devils. I must save…"

"The…the…the… if the devils come, what can we do? We…"

"I won't leave. I really have to… I really have to…"

"You can't leave either!"

"You… You…" Little Wang's face was covered in tears. "I'm

done for..."

"If you leave, who will get me dough noodle soup ... don't worry, I'm here. I..."

But that one didn't heed, he broke into a run and fled.

"Little Wang! Little Wang!" Shi Zhaochang called out shrilly. "Dammit, dammit!"

Suddenly, heaven and earth started spinning. Shi Zhaochang closed his eyes and tried to gather himself, then slowly returned home.

"Elder Brother and Elder Brother Disciple still haven't come. Thirteenth Sister still hasn't come. And I still don't have a stealth suit."

Shi Zhaochang tried to sit down on the sofa, but his butt slipped and he landed on the ground. Patterns spun around in front of his eyes like the tri-colored patterned pole in front of a barber shop. Then comet-like things joyously spun around him.

He chewed on a Golden Pill. Sweet, soft and banana flavored. But he tasted a little bitterness at the tip of his tongue.

"What do I do? I... I must... I must..."

For some reason at that moment he couldn't think of anything at all. Comets and patterns danced around so much his head throbbed. It felt like his body was floating in mid-air. He was on a cloud dais. His feet trod on variegated vapor. He saw...

"Oh, Master!"

At Master's left stood Thirteenth Sister and the Woman Warrior of National Salvation. Close on his right were Elder Brother and Elder Brother Disciple.

"What!" Shi Zhaochang spoke mostly through his nose. "Men stand to the left and women to the right. How could these two women stand to Master's left?"

The Woman Warrior of National Salvation floated to his lap.

"This is the new morality la!"

In a dazzling of comets, everyone disappeared.

Thirteenth Sister was at his side. She did a handstand, hands on the ground, her two bound-dumpling feet pointing at the ceiling. She looked at him, and he told her in a flood of words—his own story. He spoke with a great effort, as if there was a piece of iron in his throat preventing his voice from coming out. Thirteenth Sister was quiet the whole time, staying in her handstand without moving a muscle, focusing on listening to him.

The story wasn't short. He spoke for quite a while before falling silent. Actually the story ended with a cliffhanger, but the piece of iron in his throat swelled and lengthened so that no sound could come out. His tongue also became as stiff as a stone...

Shi Zhaochang passed out. The gunfire and sound of shells were getting louder outside, but Shi Zhachang slept on all the way until night without moving.

At daybreak, the shellfire was truly terrible. Shi Zhaochang shouted out wildly, his hands madly clawing at the ground. He jumped up and rushed all around the room. From the window he ran to the doorway, then from the doorway, he darted to the opposite wall. Only after tripping over the shards of a shattered vase and falling to the ground did he come completely awake.

His legs wouldn't support him. Leaning on the wall he made his way to the sofa and sat down, panting with the effort.

Outside, everything was in flames.

Boom! Crash!

The house shook.

Shi Zhaochang licked his lips. His lips were bitter.

"They still haven't come…" He closed his eyes.

Boom! Boom! Ratta-tatta-tatta-tat!

Then from far away the sound of airplanes came nearer.

"Attend me to save…" Shi Zhaochang lightly moved his lips. "But wait…"

All of a sudden there was a sound like the world exploding. The house did a summersault.

Shi Zhaochang was blown from the sofa to the ground. His ears rang—droning…

Black smoke billowed in through the window.

He started crawling, rushing outside. He couldn't see anything. In one breath he had run several blocks before gradually slowing down.

A wall collapsed in front of him. He crawled up to the pile of roof tiles and bricks and lay down like he was getting into bed. His body was like a foreign wax candle in an oven—he couldn't keep upright no matter what.

Shi Zhaochang lay there for four or five hours.

"There's an unconscious civilian there!"

"Hey! Hey!"

"Are you injured?"

"I'm not… I'm not…" Shi Zhaochang mumbled.

"Hey! Hey!" Someone helped Shi Zhaochang up.

"What!" Shi Zhaochang opened his eyes.

Eh, to lie down on a place like this!

Collapsed walls, crumbled walls, tiles, bricks, smoke, scorched timbers, soldiers and civilians running around. There were some soldiers reclining on a pile of tiles and bricks in front of him. Their rifles were pointing out, but they didn't open fire. They were just chatting with their buddies. Closer to him, a machine gun was set up next to a crumbled wall with several soldiers looking outward. Opposite gunshots rang out without cease, the bullets whizzing over.

"Why don't they open fire over here? Why… Why…"

But everything was hazy, like they were separated by a pane of frosted glass. He couldn't think straight. It was like he was walking on cotton, each step sinking in. His body sunk down too. He didn't know where he was now, and he didn't know what he had to do. His body was grabbed and taken away like some magic had taken control of him. He couldn't struggle free—no, he simply never thought to struggle free.

He forced his eyes open.

Shi Zhaochang stared, and his body went cold.

Was he mistaken? No. It absolutely had to be that…

He recognized the three civilians in front of him, no mistake. No matter what, he could never forget their faces. How—It was precisely those evil guys that he had fought at the door of the theatre! That Hou… Hou…

That Hou Changchun was staring right at him! He wanted to get into a stance and grapple with them, but he couldn't move.

Evil guys were on the firing fine too! How, he, Shi Zhaochang, had gone to save evil guys, to stand next to these unpardonable bastards!

"I won't… I must, I must…"

The firing from the opposite side grew thicker, like hail. The men supporting him dragged him with all they could, and he took advantage of this to make his move, jumping into his stance. But his knees and ankles gave out and he sunk down. Luckily, the Evil guys at his side held him up.

"Evil guys… battle magic… Master save me!"

The devil soldiers in front of him moved toward him step by step, bullets firing from the muzzles of their rifles without stop.

Suddenly the machine gun by the crumbled wall started to bark out: the rat-a-tat-a-tat rattled everyone numb.

Shi Zhaochang shouted out something, but the sound of the machine gun drowned it out. The veins popped out on his face and his mouth just opened and closed, just like a silent movie.

The soldiers who had been covered behind the pile of tiles and bricks jumped up and rushed over.

"Kill! Kill!"

"Kill! ah! Throw them back!"

"Kill!"

But Shi Zhaochang had been dragged far away

"Damn, dammit!"

Those Evil guys still had him held tightly between them, their legs never stopping. They ran all the way.

Dang: He had been captured by the evil guys!

"Master! Master!"

Shi Zhaochang struggled and broke free from their grasp. He rocked downward until his butt was on the ground.

There was no time to lose, but his head was going numb, and his ears were ringing. Who knows if they were still firing, or if he had gotten tinnitus? What the fuck does that matter, out fly the sword! He fumbled his little sword out of his pocket, and with a trembling lip, he mumbled something with a 'Fly!" as he threw the sword out.

Friends! Right then, those XX devils and those evil bastards who captured him would be in for it now.

He touched his icy-cold fingers to his boiling-hot forehead.

Ping! The sword fell in front of him.

Shi Zhaochang didn't see it. He just did his all to crawl up, moment by moment. He lifted his hand, waiting for the thrown sword to return to him.

But after so long, it didn't return. The hand he raised started to shiver and ache. Shi Zhaochang began to get light-headed again… He couldn't remember why he raised his hand up like that in the first place. What was that all about?

Bang!

His body spun like a tornado, and he fell back to the ground.

"Pass through Earth to the capital of the devil pass through… pass through… pass though…"

Black patterns again. Dancing comets again. Unable to think anything through again.

Blood flowed from his shoulder. His silk gown was completely red.

"This guy's caught a stray bullet!"

"Get over here!"

Only after Shi Zhaochang opened his eyes did he realize those evil guys really did capture him away to… Where? Heaven knows. Perhaps to some evil monk's…

Ensorcelled. No doubt. He couldn't think of anything, only close his eyes in befuddlement.

He didn't know how long he was out. He let the two evil guys drag him off without any awareness at all.

This warrior had fallen into such trouble! Master never had any flash of insight, and never figured it out, and he never dispatched Elder Brother and Elder Brother Disciple to save him.

Shi Zhaochang opened his eyes for a second time and groaned.

Sunlight dazzled his eyes.

"What…"

Where was this place? He was lying on a bed. A few people stood next to the bed—clad in white helmets and white armor.

"Evil cave... evil cave..." The evil guys captured him and had taken him to an evil cave, and it wasn't just him. There were so many beds in rows. White sheets and white mattresses, on each bed was a person.

"Save me, Master! ... Master..."

He wanted to jump up, but didn't have enough strength. There was pain in his left shoulder. Ah, it was wrapped tight in a white binding.

Raising his eyes higher—A friendly-faced woman was watching him.

Those people in white helmets and white armor mumbled together a while, looked at him, then slowly walked away.

He reached out to the woman, but his left shoulder was wrapped up tight so he couldn't. He only had use of his right arm:

"White-clad Guanyin... White-clad Guanyin..."

Perhaps she was Xuan Nü of the Nine Heavens. He looked at her carefully and altered his address: "Goddess Xuan Nü save me, Goddess Xuan Nü... Evil forces have... They... heretical sects... They..."

That Goddess Xuan Nü said nothing at all. She just pulled out a brilliant gleaming glass dagger and popped it into his mouth.

"Goddess Xuan Nü..." With the glass dagger halfway in Shi Zhaochang's mouth, speaking was strangely indistinct. "I made an oath, I... Before Emperor Lord Guan...I've been useless...Shi Zhaochang, this... My master taught me... to assist... Elder Brother and Elder Brother Disciple would assist me... The Woman Warrior of National Salvation... Thirteenth Sister... Liu Zhao and the rest..."

Shi Zhaochang pled for the Goddess Xuan Nü to save him, but there was a man with a white helmet and white armor and wearing glasses—he divined Shi Zhaochang would have to wait a month or more before his fate would throw off its baleful star.

"A month or more before he will be able..." he said to Mister Shi Boxiang. "He's not out of danger. After the surgery, his temperature wasn't high at all..."

The Elder Mister Shi Boxiang sighed, complaining that this eldest son of his was really too muddle-headed. If he hadn't mumbled out Mr. Liu Liu's address so that the hospital could send someone out to find him, he wouldn't have even known he had fallen into such trouble.

He pulled out that handkerchief that was folded into a rectangle and carelessly wiped the wisps of his beard. Then he sighed again and left to take a rickshaw to a house.

"How is it that Master Shi comes so late?" The first to great him was a bald head—eyelids covering so that the eyes couldn't look up, mouth, teeth, nose, all pulled downward. With a glance he recognized Elder Brother Disciple Ban Tuzi.

The room was crammed with people, but it was quiet. Hu Genbao smiled a greeting at The Elder Mister Shi such that his face was nothing but wrinkles. Then he quickly pulled his face very sober and stood with all propriety, staring at the desk in front of him. Even venting anger was soft and without a sound.

Kuai Sixteen and that one with the singed beard stood next to the table holding the T-shaped stick and drawing wildly in the sand box.

They were asking Ancestor Lu—When did he think the fighting in Shanghai would reach a conclusion.

The Supreme Ultimate Master stood respectfully, eyes set on the sand box. He would occasionally glance at someone, then occasionally pick at the flowing rheum in the corner of his eyes with his long black fingernail.

An hour passed like this, and then Shi Boxiang knelt in front of the table and asked when his eldest son would recover.

The T-shaped stick swooshed and scraped through the sand in the box:

"Seven by seven is forty-nine, the jug has old wine. Nine by nine is eighty-one, shiny lacquer paint won't run."

Incomprehensible.

But The Supreme Ultimate Master Understood.

"The meaning is clear. His mother couldn't hide it from me, The Supreme Ultimate Master, but... but... The secrets of heaven are not to be divulged... It says simply forty-nine days. If not, then eighty-one days. Of course... of course..."

Shi Zhaochang of course needed more than a month to recover. In that period there would probably not be any accidents: Why don't we just let him take his rest there. To use a phrase found in novels, "Let's say no more of that and turn to another subject." So—*The Classic of Poetry* says...

No. As Shi Zhaochang slept, he still recalled some people. He was always speaking in his dreams:

"Warrior Woman of National Salvation cast off Evil... cast off... Come quickly Thirteenth Sister, you... Liu Zhao wants donations, wants me... Shi Zhaowu that scoundrel, always... His mother really... really..."

Oh yeah, what of these characters? Thirteenth Sister for example?

Thirteenth Sister—no one knows what happened to her, just like at the end of gongfu stories when they say, "And nothing more was heard of them."

Elder Brother Hu Genbao never looked into any of it, as if he forgot about the whole thing.

The Woman Warrior of National Salvation went on in as

usual: Chatting about the new modern morality with several men. A person hasta care about the new morality la. And recently she had put together a new opera la. It's called *The Beauty Destroys the XX Devils* la. It's the bee's knees la.

Finally, as for Liu Zhao, he never planned to get Shi Zhaochang to donate ever again, but every evening he would go to the balcony and look north. Pointing at the glowing fires, he would chat and laugh with people. The rest of the time he played mahjong with Mister Liu Liu, Mrs. Liu and Mrs. Shi.

"Mrs. Shi Bo, give me an eight."

Whenever Mrs. Shi sat down at the mahjong table, she had to look carefully at the other three faces, suspicious that they might just be buttering her up. All her attention was on the tiles. But there was always something to distract her:

"Ma! Brother pinched me..."

"Mistress, just you look at Second Young Master—he ran off with my vest..."

Mrs. Shi sighed loudly, shaking her head, immediately shaking the hair away that had been covering the purple scar on her temple.

"Zhaowu! Zhaowu! ... Boxiang! ... Really, he's run off again. You tell me, how I am supposed to be able to play? Such a nuisance! Wet nurse first can't hold onto her pants, now she can't hold onto her vest. But you are too... too... What are you beating Fourth Sister for? Just hauling off and hitting her. Fine slap your tiles down: slap down a good one and I'll take it. I never seem to draw a long set here, it's just all over the place. Never any good luck. With no good luck, it's no wonder I'm playing so wild. People with bad luck always play wild, but you shouldn't hit Fourth Sister, you should go off and hit the XX! But he hasn't gotten his military rank this year, right, ah, Mrs. Liu, isn't that so. How am I supposed to be able to play like this, really! Just make me into a jumble, ah, a real jumble. Just going off and hitting fourth sister, don't you think that's a jumble, and jumbled up as Zhaochang. Zhaochang, that child… You all don't look at him as a twenty or thirty year old adult man, there's still a lot of things he doesn't understand, hahaha, Oh, it really kills me. One day he… One day he… hahaha Oh! It just really kills me. Haha! Oh it's so funny, look, play a pair of south winds, isn't that funny? My luck is really bad today. Ordinarily my luck isn't great. Before, when I was at school, hm, I would always win at mahjong. Win? My family practically didn't have to put up any tuition. My English teacher played often, too. He said that the Emperor of the United States promoted mahjong, even with that promoting, our eldest doesn't smack down the tiles. He only hits the walls, swings his fists, plops himself down for meditation… even when a cracking war starts up, he doesn't leave, and now—now do you hear the tiles? Mrs. Liu? I haven't heard them, I… I…"